CAMPFIRE TALES

CAMPFIRE TALES

Ghoulies, Ghosties, and Long-Leggety Beasties

Third Edition

WILLIAM W. FORGEY
Illustrated by Paul G. Hoffman

FALCONGUIDES

GUILFORD, CONNECTICUT
HELENA, MONTANA

AN IMPRINT OF ROWMAN & LITTLEFIELD

To Ralph, Bobby, David, and Christopher Ehresman—may we always remember our time together in the "deep, dark woods," and may you continue to have many adventures in the great outdoors.

From ghoulies and ghosties and long-leggety beasties
And things that go bump in the night,
Good Lord, deliver us.

Cornish Prayer

CONTENTS

ACKNOWLEDGMENTS

My exposure to storytelling came about because of my three Scout troops and later because of my many friends with whom I have shared the canoeing and winter trails of the far north. I appreciate their enthusiasm for more and more stories over the years. I gratefully recognize the research and editorial assistance of Patrick Sherwood, a scoutmaster who has provided many youth with memorable campfire programs.

INTRODUCTION

How to Tell, and Find, a Ghost Story

In my first book, *Campfire Stories,* I discussed the creation
of the storytelling portion of a campfire program—with
helpful hints on setting the proper mood, the ideal physical surroundings, and the techniques of storytelling.

These hints were so well received that I decided to
share them with you here:

- Enjoy and have fun telling the story, be relaxed,
  and don't be afraid to "ham it up" a little, perhaps
  at times making a fool of yourself. Being stiff,
  formal, or even worried about the story will be
  noticeably distracting and make your listeners
  uncomfortable.

- Maintain eye contact with your audience. This
  absolutely precludes reading a story. Memorize
  the story well enough that you can tell it
  without referring to notes or in any other way
  distracting from the intensity of the story. I
  probably never tell the same story exactly the
  same way twice. Get the general facts down and
  then improvise as necessary to keep the story
  moving smoothly.

- Be in close physical contact with your audience—the closer the better. Avoid standing on a stage or behind a podium. Close contact is much easier to maintain in small groups than large ones. You have to make up for distance when the group is large with increased personal intensity and magnetism—not always an easy order. Especially at first, keep the group small.

- Do not get hung up on details—yet it is details that can give a story its authenticity. Try not to get tripped up on names, dates, or other "facts," as children are quick to notice these discrepancies. There is certainly nothing wrong with making up these finishing touches as you go along. Each story in this book has an outline, giving details of names and other facts that can be changed by the storyteller. I will frequently use names to provide reality at the beginning of the story—then if I have forgotten which name went with which character as the story unfolds, I simply work around this mental block, calling the character by some other description (young man, old man, hunter, prospector, his friend, and so on).

- Set a quiet mood before beginning your storytelling session. I find that tired audiences are best. Keep your camping group active during the day. The properly constructed evening program consumes extra energy and then quiets the audience down; it puts your listeners into a reflective and receptive mood. This is a must, or the storytelling should be put off to some other day. It is unfair to yourself or other members of the group to tell a story when other members are uncooperative or rowdy.

• A campfire program is an ideal storytelling medium. It is the perfect vehicle to use up that energy that young audiences have in such large quantities. As the campfire starts, the program should include active-participation parts with skits, songs, stunts—all designed to include every audience member. Storytelling by youngsters has to be limited because it can sometimes drag terribly. Instead they can be involved in physically setting up the program and helping to run it. Many fine books on organizing and running campfires, with suggestions for themes, can be found in bookstores or at camping outfitters. The end of the campfire, after the embers have burned down low, is the perfect time to tell a scary story.

• While it is possible to have a story session, even a "campfire program," without a real campfire, build one if at all possible. Who cannot help but feel a mystical sense of awareness when staring at the flames of a campfire? Who hasn't placed a stick in a fire, stirred the coals, and watched the swirling embers move skyward, pondering the mysteries of the universe? With a small group you can allow this. In a bigger group, generally you'll build a larger fire and the embers will blaze skyward on their own. Regardless, a fire can play a very important part in setting the mood for a memorable storytelling session.

- It is totally unnecessary when telling an intense and scary story to use props or to have a secret agent assist you by jumping out of the woods or dressing up in a strange fashion. In fact shenanigans of that nature distract from the basic story and take away from its credibility.

- Use different inflections of voice to add moments of fear or excitement to your story. Tell your story with intensity and direct contact. At a certain point in the story, when you know that the victim or person in the story might let out a scream, break through the intensity with a sudden shout or scream. With proper timing, everyone listening will literally lift about two inches off his or her seat.

- Really good scary stories need credibility. A ghost story that features a detached hand crawling along the floor, trying to strangle its victims, might be entertaining, but it will not fulfill the request for a memorable scary story. If you start your storytelling session with true or believable tales, the audience will be held in your grasp, spellbound.

The real challenge, then, is finding the scary stories that kids always seem to request. When you do find suitable stories, they generally fall into two classifications: One is the perfect story that helps set the mood, and the second group includes those stories that benefit from being told after a top-notch tale. The perfect story can be told to a group that is only half cooperative, or perhaps a little too large, or too old in age. I would consider a story like "The Graveyard Rats" (or "The Diamond Stickpin" version) to be in this category. Once you have your listeners' attention, then they are on your side. They are in a cooperative mood and then most any story will hold their attention.

Where does one find a good story line? Surprisingly, anthologies of occult tales yield very little that you can use. Generally they are too long or rely on complex descriptions to bring about their effect. And while they make good reading, they are too difficult to remember in detail and tell. But there is the occasional gem.

Folklore books, old scary comic books, collections of short stories, adventure stories, even books of poetry can lend you a story line that can be modified into the campfire story that you are seeking. There is the very occasional TV program that provides a scary theme for campfire use. Campfire program books usually offer stories with a humorous basis, Indian lore, or obviously juvenile stories. Parks and recreation department programs are very good sources. You will need to check local county, state, and national parks—particularly around Halloween—to see if they are having a "graveyard" story session. Local parks will also stage programs during festivals around special events or local folklore legends that might provide very useful story material. Local camps are a fine source of classic campfire tales, too. Camp counselors are always willing to trade yarns, for their benefit as well as yours.

If the story is well chosen, the delivery does not have to be all that polished. In fact I have tried to include stories that lend themselves well to the telling, and I have indicated how to go about finding and modifying other stories for your own use.

So come along with me and chase ghoulies from a deep, dark grave; vindicate the misdeeds of a deranged madman; look over your shoulder for mysterious movements in the dark; travel in time to an Asian jungle; and discover swamps with eerie creatures from the night.

1

THE GRAVEYARD RATS

by Henry Kuttner

This story started my storytelling career. While still a youngster, I read a story in one of the horror comics that stuck with me. Many years later, when taking my first Scout troop camping, the boys asked me for a story. I told for the first time a tale I called "The Story of the Cemetery Rats." It was a rousing sensation. Oh, it attracted no applause, only silence around the campfire when I was finished. But the oldest boy asked if he and the other big guys, who had pitched camp off by themselves, could grab their gear and join me and the younger guys that night. I knew that I had hit home.

Many years later, hoping to find a suitable campfire story, I was going through an anthology of supernatural stories when I came across the original version. Occasionally one of these stories is a real gem and is easily adapted to storytelling. "The Graveyard Rats" by Henry Kuttner, which is reproduced here, is such a gem.

Old Masson, the caretaker of one of Salem's oldest and most-neglected cemeteries, had a feud with the rats. Generations ago they had come up from the wharves and settled in the graveyard, a colony of abnormally large rats, and when Masson had taken charge after the inexplicable disappearance of the former caretaker, he decided that they must go. At first he set traps for them and put poisoned food by their burrows, and later he tried to shoot them, but it did no good. The rats stayed, multiplying and over-running the graveyard with their ravenous hordes.

They were large, even for the *Mus decumanus,* which sometimes measures fifteen inches in length, exclusive of the naked pink and gray tail. Masson had caught glimpses of some as large as good-size cats, and when, once or twice, the grave diggers had uncovered their burrows, the malodorous tunnels were large enough to enable a man to crawl into them on his hands and knees. The ships that had come generations ago from distant ports to the rotting Salem wharves had brought strange cargoes.

Masson wondered sometimes at the extraordinary size of these burrows. He recalled certain vaguely disturbing legends he had heard since coming to ancient, witch-haunted Salem—tales of a moribund, inhuman life that was said to exist in forgotten burrows in the earth. The old days, when Cotton Mather had hunted down the evil cults that worshiped Hecate and the dark Magna Mater in frightful orgies, had passed; but dark, gabled houses still leaned perilously toward each other over narrow cobbled streets, and blasphemous secrets and mysteries were said to be hidden in subterranean cellars and caverns, where forgotten pagan rites were still celebrated in defiance of law and sanity. Wagging their gray heads wisely, the elders declared that there were worse things than rats and maggots crawling in the unhallowed earth of the ancient Salem cemeteries.

And then, too, there was this curious dread of the rats. Masson disliked and respected the ferocious little rodents, for he knew the danger that lurked in their flashing, needle-sharp fangs; but he could not understand the inexplicable horror that the oldsters held for deserted, rat-infested houses. He had heard vague rumors of ghoulish beings that dwelt far underground, and that had the power of commanding the rats, marshaling them like horrible armies. The rats, the old men whispered, were messengers between this world and the grim and ancient caverns far below Salem. Bodies had been stolen from graves for nocturnal subterranean feasts, they said. The myth of the Pied Piper is a fable that hides a blasphemous horror, and the black pits of Avernus have brought forth hell-spawned monstrosities that never venture into the light of day.

Masson paid little attention to these tales. He did not fraternize with his neighbors, and, in fact, did all he could to hide the existence of the rats from intruders.

Investigation, he realized, would undoubtedly mean the opening of many graves. And while some of the gnawed, empty coffins could be attributed to the activities of the rats, Masson might find it difficult to explain the mutilated bodies that lay in some of the coffins. The purest gold is used in filling teeth, and this gold is not removed when a man is buried. Clothing, of course, is another matter; for usually the undertaker provides a plain broadcloth suit that is cheap and easily recognizable. Sometimes, too, there were medical students and less reputable doctors who were in need of cadavers, and not overscrupulous as to where these were obtained.

So far Masson had successfully managed to discourage investigation. He had fiercely denied the existence of the rats, even though they sometimes robbed him of his prey. Masson did not care what happened to the bodies after he had performed his gruesome thefts, but the rats inevitably dragged away the whole cadaver through the hole they gnawed in the coffin.

The size of these burrows occasionally worried Masson. Then, too, there was the curious circumstance of the coffins always being gnawed open at the end, never at the side or top. It was almost as though the rats were working under the direction of some impossibly intelligent leader.

Now he stood in an open grave and threw a last sprinkling of wet earth on the heap beside the pit. It was raining a slow, cold drizzle that for weeks had been descending from soggy black clouds. The graveyard was a slough of yellow, sucking mud from which the rain-washed tombstones stood up in irregular battalions. The rats had retreated to their burrows, and Masson had not seen one for days. But his gaunt, unshaven face was set in frowning lines; the coffin on which he was standing was a wooden one. The body had been buried several days earlier, but Masson had not dared to disinter it before. A relative of the dead man had been coming to the grave at intervals, even in the drenching rain. But he would hardly come at this late hour, no matter how much grief he might be suffering, Masson thought, grinning wryly. He straightened and laid the shovel aside.

From the hill on which the ancient graveyard lay he could see the lights of Salem flickering dimly through the downpour. He drew a flashlight from his pocket. He would need light now. Taking up the spade, he bent and examined the fastenings of the coffin.

Abruptly he stiffened. Beneath his feet he sensed an unquiet stirring and scratching, as though something were moving within the coffin. For a moment a pang of superstitious fear shot through Masson, and then rage replaced it as he realized the significance of the sound. The rats had forestalled him again!

In a paroxysm of anger, Masson wrenched at the fastenings of the coffin. He got the sharp edge of the shovel under the lid and pried it up until he could finish the job with his hands. Then he sent the flashlight's cold beam darting down into the coffin.

Rain spattered against the white satin lining; the coffin was empty. Masson saw a flicker of movement at the head of the case and darted the light in that direction.

The end of the sarcophagus had been gnawed through, and a gaping hole led into darkness. A black shoe, limp and dragging, was disappearing as Masson watched, and abruptly he realized that the rats had forestalled him by only a few minutes. He fell on his hands and knees and made a hasty clutch at the shoe, and the flashlight inconveniently fell into the coffin and went out. The shoe was tugged from his grasp, he heard a sharp, excited squealing, and then he had the flashlight again and was darting its light into the burrow.

It was a large one. It had to be, or the corpse could not have been dragged along it. Masson wondered at the size of the rats that could carry away a man's body, but the thought of the loaded revolver in his pocket fortified him. Probably if the corpse had been an ordinary one, Masson would have left the rats with their spoils rather than venture into the narrow burrow, but he remembered an especially fine set of cuff links he had observed, as well as a stickpin that was undoubtedly a genuine pearl. With scarcely a pause he clipped the flashlight to his belt and crept into the burrow.

It was a tight fit, but he managed to squeeze himself along. Ahead of him in the flashlight's glow he could see the shoes dragging along the wet earth of the bottom of the tunnel. He crept along the burrow as rapidly as he could, occasionally barely able to squeeze his lean body through the narrow walls.

The air was overpowering with its musty stench of carrion. If he could not reach the corpse in a minute, Masson decided, he would turn back. Belated fears were beginning to crawl, maggotlike, within his mind, but greed urged him on. He crawled forward, several times passing the mouths of adjoining tunnels. The walls of the burrow were damp and slimy, and twice lumps of dirt dropped behind him. The second time he paused and screwed his head around to look back. He could see nothing, of course, until he had unhooked the flashlight from his belt and reversed it.

Several clods lay on the ground behind him, and the danger of his position suddenly became real and terrifying. With thoughts of a cave-in making his pulse race, he decided to abandon the pursuit, even though he had now almost overtaken the corpse and the invisible things that pulled it. But he had overlooked one thing: The burrow was too narrow to allow him to turn.

Panic touched him briefly, but he remembered a side tunnel he had just passed and backed awkwardly along the tunnel until he came to it. He thrust his legs into it, backing until he found himself able to turn. Then he hurriedly began to retrace his way, although his knees were bruised and painful.

Agonizing pain shot through his leg. He felt sharp teeth sink into his flesh and kicked out frantically. There was a shrill squealing and the scurry of many feet. Flashing the light behind him, Masson caught his breath in a sob of fear as he saw a dozen great rats watching him intently, their slitted eyes glittering in the light. They were great misshapen things, as large as cats, and behind them he caught a glimpse of a dark shape that stirred and moved swiftly aside into the shadow; and he shuddered at the unbelievable size of the thing.

The light had held them for a moment, but they were edging closer, their teeth dull orange in pale light. Masson tugged at his pistol, managed to extricate it from his pocket, and aimed carefully. It was an awkward position,

The Graveyard Rats

and he tried to press his feet into the soggy sides of the burrow so that he should not inadvertently send a bullet into one of them.

The rolling thunder of the shot deafened him, for a time, and the clouds of smoke set him coughing. When he could hear again and the smoke had cleared, he saw that the rats were gone. He put the pistol back and began to creep swiftly along the tunnel, and then with a scurry and a rush they were upon him again.

They swarmed over his legs, biting and squealing insanely, and Masson shrieked horribly as he snatched for his gun. He fired without aiming, and only luck saved him from blowing off a foot. This time the rats did not retreat so far, but Masson was crawling as swiftly as he could along the burrow, ready to fire again at the first sound of another attack.

There was a patter of feet, and he sent the light stabbing in back of him. A great gray rat paused and watched him. Its long ragged whiskers twitched, and its scabrous, naked tail was moving slowly from side to side. Masson shouted, and the rat retreated.

He crawled on, pausing briefly, the black gap of a side tunnel at his elbow, as he made out a shapeless huddle on the damp clay a few yards ahead. For a second he thought it was a mass of earth that had been dislodged from the roof, and then he recognized it as a human body.

It was a brown and shriveled mummy, and with a dreadful unbelieving shock Masson realized that it was moving.

It was crawling toward him, and in the pale glow of the flashlight the man saw a frightful gargoyle face thrust into his own. It was the passionless, death's-head skull of a long-dead corpse, instinct with hellish life; and the glazed eyes swollen and bulbous betrayed the thing's blindness. It made a faint groaning sound as it crawled toward Masson, stretching its ragged and granulated lips in a grin of dreadful hunger. And Masson was frozen with abysmal fear and loathing.

Just before the Horror touched him, Masson flung himself frantically into the burrow at his side. He heard a scrambling noise at his heels, and the thing groaned dully as it came after him. Masson, glancing over his shoulder, screamed and propelled himself desperately through the narrow burrow. He crawled along awkwardly, sharp stones cutting his hands and knees. Dirt showered into his eyes, but he dared not pause even for a moment. He scrambled on, gasping, cursing, and praying hysterically.

Squealing triumphantly, the rats came at him, horrible hunger in their eyes. Masson almost succumbed to their vicious teeth before he succeeded in beating them off. The passage was narrowing, and in a frenzy of terror he kicked and screamed and fired until the hammer clicked on an empty shell. But he had driven them off.

He found himself crawling under a great stone, embedded in the roof, that dug cruelly into his back. It moved a little as his weight struck it, and an idea flashed into Masson's fright-crazed mind. If he could bring down the stone so that it blocked the tunnel!

The earth was wet and soggy from the rains, and he hunched himself half upright and dug away at the dirt around the stone. The rats were coming closer. He saw their eyes glowing in the reflection of the flashlight's beam. Still he clawed frantically at the earth. The stone was giving. He tugged at it, and it rocked in its foundation.

A rat was approaching—the monster he had already glimpsed. Gray and leprous and hideous it crept forward with its orange teeth bared, and in its wake came the blind dead thing, groaning as it crawled. Masson gave a last frantic tug at the stone. He felt it slide downward, and then he went scrambling along the tunnel.

Behind him the stone crashed down, and he heard a sudden frightful shriek of agony. Clods showered upon his legs. A heavy weight fell on his feet, and he dragged them free with difficulty. The entire tunnel was collapsing!

Gasping with fear, Masson threw himself forward as the soggy earth collapsed at his heels. The tunnel narrowed until he could barely use his hands and legs to propel himself; he wriggled forward like an eel and suddenly felt satin tearing beneath his clawing fingers, and then his head crashed against something that barred his path. He moved his legs, discovering that they were pinned under the collapsed earth. He was lying flat on his stomach, and when he tried to raise himself, he found that the roof was only a few inches from his back. Panic shot through him.

When the blind horror had blocked his path, he had flung himself desperately into a side tunnel, a tunnel that had no outlet. He was in a coffin, an empty coffin into which he had crept through the hole the rats had gnawed in its end!

He tried to turn on his back and found that he could not. The lid of the coffin pinned him down inexorably. Then he braced himself and strained at the coffin lid. It was immovable, and even if he could escape from the sarcophagus, how could he claw his way up through five feet of hard-packed earth?

He found himself gasping. It was dreadfully fetid, unbearably hot. In a paroxysm of terror, he ripped and clawed at the satin until it was shredded. He made a futile attempt to dig with his feet at the earth from the collapsed burrow that blocked his retreat. If he were only able to reverse his position he might be able to claw his way through to air . . . air . . . .

White-hot agony lanced through his breast, throbbed in his eyeballs. His head seemed to be swelling, growing larger and larger; and suddenly he heard the exultant squealing of the rats. He began to scream insanely but could not drown them out. For a moment he thrashed about hysterically within his narrow prison, and then he was quiet, gasping for air. His eyelids closed, his blackened tongue protruded, and he sank down into the blackness of death with the mad squealing of the rats dinning in his ears.

And thus ends one of the really great short stories of the horror genre. As mentioned elsewhere, it would seem that books of horror stories would be ideal sources for campfire tales. But, alas, this is not the case. Henry Kuttner's tale "The Graveyard Rats" is certainly an exception.

At the end of each story, throughout the remainder of this book, there will be a story outline in large type to facilitate refreshing your memory about the story, even by the dull and flickering light of a campfire. In this instance, however, the following tale demonstrates how the Kuttner story could be better adapted to storytelling for an audience in its early or mid-teens. I have found from years of experience that credible story lines have a much more profound impact. In fact when introducing this tale, I often cite old newspaper clippings from a New England town as being the source and present it as a factual event.

2

THE DIAMOND STICKPIN

by Doc Forgey

My version of the story "The Graveyard Rats" is titled "The Diamond Stickpin." This story emphasizes the evil character of the undertaker and establishes his strong desire to obtain a diamond stickpin that was buried on a corpse. It further shows how greed lured him into the tunnels of the cemetery rats, where he met his doom by backing into the wrong tunnel and being consumed. What follows is an adaptation of Henry Kuttner's story, "The Graveyard Rats."

In New England, which has many towns founded during early colonial days, there are cemeteries that are hundreds of years old. Down in the depths of this ground, cemetery rats live. The rats live in huge caves, which they have hollowed out with connecting tunnels throughout the cemetery. When someone is being buried, the rats can sense the digging from the vibrations, and they start gnawing a feeder tunnel. The feeder tunnel is dug until it connects to the new coffin that has been placed in the ground. They would then gnaw through that coffin—gnawing their way into the body's last resting place—and then eat that human body!

Many years ago in a New England town, there was a greedy undertaker. Even worse, the undertaker was actually a grave robber. And what an advantage he had! Before burying someone, he would steal all of his or her jewelry. If the body had gold teeth or silver fillings, he would pull them out. And he would take the jewelry from the fingers. He would then remove the valuable stones and melt the metals from the teeth and rings into precious ingots of pure gold, platinum, and silver. And he would bag the jewels into little parcels of sapphires, diamonds, rubies, emeralds, and pearls.

Over the years he accumulated great wealth in the vault hidden in one corner of his embalming room basement. Oh, he had great plans for his wealth. He wanted to retire to a South American country where he could live like a king, with servants, a mansion, and all of the finer things in life that he could imagine. And so he slaved away in the dark funeral home basement, hoarding his precious things, all valuables stolen from the dead.

But greed always has its own special method of destruction for those who harbor it. This man, who was already worth a fortune, knew of one thing in that town that he wanted more than any other object he had stolen. And that item was a beautiful diamond stickpin.

A stickpin is a piece of jewelry that was very popular in the olden days. It consists of a straight pin that is used to carefully tack a tie down against the wearer's shirt. Of course one had to be careful not to stick one's self with it, and for perhaps that reason stickpins are no longer popular. On the heads of these pins, people would very often place an item of great value to them, such as club emblems or even beautiful gemstones. One particular old man placed a very beautiful blue diamond on the head of his stickpin—it was worth a fortune, and it was spectacular. The greedy old undertaker felt that he had to have that diamond stickpin!

He also had another plan for stealing gems. In case he did not get to bury someone who had an item he wanted, he would go to the funeral to see if the item was being buried with the body in the casket. If it was, that night he would go to the cemetery while the grave was fresh and the ground still loose and easy to dig. Under the cover of darkness, he would then dig and rob that grave. Afterward he would pile the dirt back on. People knew there was a grave robber at work, but they could never catch him. Sometimes he would strike the next night, sometimes he would wait two or three nights—but always while the moon was dark and the fog was thick enough to cover his nefarious activity.

The old man who owned the diamond stickpin had a suspicion about the undertaker. When the greedy undertaker asked him if he could perform the funeral service for him, when it was needed, the old man said, "No, you are never going to bury me. I know what you want. You are never going to get my diamond stickpin!"

When the old man died, the undertaker went to the funeral and there, sure enough, in the coffin with the old man was that beautiful diamond stickpin! He knew that very night he wasn't going to take any chances, that he would have to rob that grave. He wanted that diamond stickpin! He did not want those cemetery rats to get in there and drag that body out of the coffin.

That night, in the swirling mist, he went out to the cemetery and started digging. He had to dig out the entire lid of that cement vault before he could open it. All of the dirt had to be out of the six-foot-deep hole. He had to work hard and fast. His fortune awaited him; South America waited for him. All that stood in his way was the huge amount of heavy earth separating him from the cement vault lid and then the coffin.

Finally he had all of the dirt off the cement lid. He lifted it up, straining with all his might. There was the coffin underneath. He took his chisel and he SMASHED the lock off the coffin . . . and . . . then he opened the lid.

BUT THERE WAS NO BODY IN IT.

Wait, there was a body—just the feet at the top of the coffin, disappearing into a tunnel as he watched. The cemetery rats had almost beat him to it! The coffin had obviously been buried close to a main tunnel. The rats were aware of a fresh body being buried very close to them, so they had made a new feeder tunnel and gnawed through the cement vault and the metal casket with their razor sharp teeth to GET THAT HUMAN BODY!

They got the body, and they were pulling it into their main tunnel. The undertaker jumped down into the coffin, grabbed hold of the feet, and tried to pull the body out so that he could get the diamond stickpin! He heaved with all of his might. But the rats were huge and powerful. They kept pulling that body farther and farther—and the undertaker was being pulled into the tunnel! But he was not going to let go of that diamond stickpin!

He had the corpse by the ankles; then he reached up higher on the corpse, grabbing up to the knees, grabbing up to the waist, pulling himself up with the dirt falling around him and the frenzied rats all around. The commotion caused by the thousands of giant cemetery rats grew and grew as they sensed a live human in among them. They were being driven crazy with a blood lust and lunged into the main tunnel from all sides. Their frenzy increased as they jumped at the undertaker's out-reached arms, lashing, gnashing, slashing at his fingers, arms, back, and legs.

He felt the pain, stabbing at him from all sides, but he desperately held on, with only one thing on his mind. Blinded by the dark and dirt, feeling sharp stabs of pain from all sides, he grabbed and grabbed higher on the corpse until HE GOT THAT DIAMOND STICKPIN!

HE HAD IT IN HIS HAND! HE HAD THAT DIAMOND STICKPIN! But he had to back up in a hurry—the rats were vicious; their stench was worse than the corpse's; their heavy bodies were slamming into him. He felt pain everywhere. His little finger was bitten off. His right ear was torn away; they were trying to reach his jugular vein and sever his windpipe! The slashing of his skin didn't hurt as much as the fear that now shot through him: He had to save his life, he had to get out of there before they ate him alive! Vicious teeth slashed at his nose and the skin on his head. He desperately backed into the tunnel, feeling rats biting at his legs, BUT HE HAD THAT DIAMOND STICKPIN. He backed into the coffin, escaping down the short feeder tunnel, he raised up, BUT . . . THE COFFIN WAS SHUT . . .

In horror he realized what had happened, he had backed into the wrong tunnel. He was trapped as thousands of rats poured into that coffin with him . . . *AAAUUUGGGHHH!*

And he died being chewed to pieces by the rats.

The next day out at the cemetery, there was an open grave with no body, the grave of the buried old man. Leading from the coffin was a tunnel. When the sheriff went out to investigate, he realized that a grave robber had been at work and had opened a coffin that the cemetery rats had also entered. There was nothing he could do about it but have concrete poured into the coffin to seal it up and fill part of the tunnel.

Two days later townspeople noticed that the old undertaker had disappeared. They broke into his office, and there they found his vault. The bags of jewels and precious metals were inside it. Now they knew who the cemetery robber had been all of those years.

Story Outline

I. An old New England graveyard has been undermined by tunnels dug by cemetery rats that gnaw their way to freshly buried bodies.

II. An evil undertaker has been stealing jewels and gold from the people he buries at the cemetery and has been digging up the graves of wealthy people for whom he does not provide services.

III. This evil man desires to obtain a beautiful diamond stickpin worn by one of the wealthy old men in the town; it would end his quest for a fortune in loot that would allow him to live like a king in South America.

IV. The wealthy old man is suspicious of the undertaker and arranges to be buried by someone else when he dies.

V. Upon the wealthy old man's death, the undertaker goes to the graveyard the night of his funeral to dig up the diamond stickpin, but when he reaches the coffin, he finds it empty—the rats had already robbed the casket of its corpse.

VI. But wait, as the undertaker drops down into the coffin, he sees the feet of the corpse disappearing into the tunnel, being dragged by the rats.

VII. The undertaker grabs the corpse by the feet and is pulled into the tunnel. He pulls himself up higher and higher onto the corpse, reaching for the diamond stickpin.

VIII. Finally, he has the diamond stickpin! But the rats begin biting him viciously. He backs up hurriedly into the coffin, but when he tries to get up—the coffin lid is down—he has backed into the wrong tunnel!

In telling the above story, I generally SMASH the lock off the coffin when the grave robber is about to open it (V above) and certainly finish with a substantial scream when he finds that he has backed into a closed coffin down the wrong tunnel. The "smash" generally causes the front row to jump about two inches in the air, and the ending gives them something really terrible to think about—being buried alive and being eaten by rats, but I do not use the theme of a crawling corpse, and I do not emphasize the supernatural aspects of the original story.

3

GOLD TOOTH

by Scott E. Power and Doc Forgey

The ideal story will not only be entertaining but also have a moral. Such is the case with this story, in which both father and son learn a variety of lessons.

One weekend Mr. Simpson and his thirteen-year-old son Jimmy were camping in the Jacksonville State Forest area. They had prepared this camp with very little help from Mom. Well, except for some advice. She saw Dad packing a large can of sauerkraut and asked him what he planned to do with it. He responded that it was for supper on Saturday night.

Mom didn't think that was a very good idea. "I know what will happen," she said. "You'll go to bed right after supper because you'll both be afraid of the dark, and

Jimmy will have horrible nightmares after eating that sauerkraut."

"Nonsense," her husband remarked and packed the sauerkraut anyway.

Friday night they went to bed early—not because they were scared, but because they were tired. They had gotten up early, finished packing, and driven half the day to reach the beautiful campsite that they were able to claim.

Saturday was a busy day. And even though they ate a good breakfast and lunch, the full day of hiking left them starving by supper time. The sauerkraut turned out to be a real treat that evening. It certainly complemented the grilled sausage! And for dessert, they enjoyed banana pudding washed down with hot chocolate.

After relaxing around the campfire a short while, they turned on their AM/FM radio to hear the news.

Unexpectedly, they heard an emergency news report over the radio:

Attention, attention, all citizens:

Just hours ago a convicted murderer escaped from the Jacksonville Correctional Center. Initial attempts to capture him have failed. He is at large and is considered dangerous. He is believed to be heading north-northwest on foot. He stands about six feet, four inches and weighs approximately 280 pounds. He has long brown hair, a beard, and a mustache. He is known by the name "Gold Tooth." If you have any knowledge of the whereabouts of this escaped criminal, please call

your local police immediately. For your own
safety, if you are camping in the Jacksonville
State Forest area, please leave immediately.

Instantly, Jimmy turned to his dad in fear.

"Don't be afraid, son. You have nothing to worry
about. Jacksonville Correctional Center is twenty miles
north over Jackson Ridge. Besides we're leaving in the
morning, and there is no way anyone could travel that
distance on foot in twelve hours. Anyway the news report
said he's traveling north-northwest, and we're due south."

"Dad, I don't care. I'm scared. I wanna go home,"
Jimmy replied.

"What if I gave you something to protect yourself with?"

"Like what, Dad, a Swiss Army knife?"

"No, of course not. I brought the rifle for a little target
practice tomorrow morning before we leave. But if you'd
like, I'll keep it in the tent tonight for protection."

"You will?"

"Yes, I will."

"Really? Do you promise?"

"Yes, I promise."

"Okay, let's stay. But I'm getting tired. I want to go to
sleep. And my stomach is acting up a little."

Jimmy got up from sitting by the campfire and walked
over to the tent and got in. Mr. Simpson walked over to
the duffel bags and began to look for the rifle, finding it
in the red one.

As he held it in his hand, Mr. Simpson knew the gun
was not loaded. And he did not plan to load it either.
Mr. Simpson had no concern whatsoever that the escaped

prisoner would threaten them in any way. He was merely providing a sense of security for his son. Mr. Simpson was more concerned about a possible bear attack than the prisoner at large.

Walking past the tent to put the fire out, Mr. Simpson noticed that Jimmy had already fallen asleep. Smiling to himself, he picked up a pail of water and poured it over the fire. Immediately the sizzle of steam rose into the air as the fire light disappeared into the darkness.

Mr. Simpson turned on his flashlight to find his way back to the tent. He held the flashlight in his right hand and the rifle in his left as he walked. After crawling into the tent, he placed the rifle between the sleeping bags. Once he zipped up the tent door behind him, Mr. Simpson crawled into his sleeping bag, zipped it up, and then turned the flashlight off. As he lay in the darkness, he could hear Jimmy snoring and the gentle noises from the crickets and bullfrogs outside. For a moment he thought about how happy he was to be in such a beautiful, peaceful place with his son, whom he loved so much. Everything was perfect. Peaceful. Serene.

Slowly, Mr. Simpson could feel himself falling asleep and beginning to dream. Soon he was deep in sleep and snoring, too.

Jimmy awoke in the middle of the night, probably around four in the morning. He was squirming because his stomach was cramped and he was having nightmares.

As he lay on his back looking up at the top of the tent, he immediately thought about the escaped murderer. He turned his head to look toward his father, and then he saw the gun between them. Instantly he was relieved. He felt safe again.

Then in the distance he heard *CRACK!*

It sounded like someone stepping on a fallen branch. Then, he heard *CRUNCH!*

It sounded like someone stepping onto a pile of leaves. Then, he heard *CRACK!* again. Another broken branch.

Jimmy tried to wake up his dad, but he couldn't. He tried shaking him, but his dad was sleeping too deeply. Jimmy grabbed the rifle and pointed it at the door, not knowing that it wasn't loaded.

Then outside the tent Jimmy saw the shape of a man silhouetted by the light of the moon. Instantly, without thought, he pulled the trigger of the unloaded gun.

POW!

The gun fired and a bullet ripped through the tent striking the shadowy figure dead.

Mr. Simpson woke up in a panic and didn't understand what had happened. Everything seemed chaotic and confusing. His ears rang from the sound of the gun's firing. He couldn't believe the gun was loaded. He thought for sure it was not. Good thing he was wrong.

Jimmy was sitting still holding the gun firmly in his grip. His eyes were locked straight ahead in the direction that he had fired. He was trembling with fear. Finally he spoke.

"I saw him. It was him. The escaped prisoner. I know it was him. He was going to kill us. I had to do it, I had to do it, I had to do it," Jimmy repeated.

Gold Tooth

Hours later, the cops arrived on the scene. The man did not look like the escaped prisoner. He had short hair, no beard or mustache, and was wearing street clothes.

Jimmy felt sick that he had shot at someone without knowing at whom he was shooting. His dad felt terrible that he had made the awful mistake of thinking that a gun was unloaded without opening the breech and checking.

Jimmy was arrested as a murderer and taken to Jacksonville Prison. There he was placed in the very cell that the escaped convict had been in.

"Kid, is this cell good enuff for ya?" a guard asked. "Ya kilt my brother-in-law, Henry. We'll just keep you here till they hang ya."

Later that night a man with long hair was brought in wearing handcuffs and leg chains. The guard laughed as he shoved him into Jimmy's cell.

"Hey, you two murderers should get along just fine in there," he cackled, as he slammed the door, locked it, and walked away down the hall leaving the two in there together.

"Aw, what are ya in for kid? Ya murda someone like me?"

As his cellmate laughed, Jimmy saw the gold tooth shining through the droopy long mustache and beard covering his face. And Jimmy realized that he was finally meeting the killer face-to-face, locked in a cell together without anyone around to help. And all because he shot someone he didn't even know.

"Say kid," Gold Tooth exclaimed as he came closer and closer to Jimmy, "I hear you be here fer tryin' to kill me."

Jimmy backed up until he was finally trapped in a corner of the cell. Gold Tooth put his manacled hands out in front of him, reaching for Jimmy.

"I hates when people tries to kill me," Gold Tooth growled, snatching Jimmy around the waist as Jimmy tried to sneak past him.

Jimmy struggled with every ounce of his energy against the overwhelming strength of Gold Tooth, but he just couldn't break away. Gold Tooth had him and wasn't letting go!

Jimmy knew he was going to die. Gold Tooth was squeezing the breath out of him. His last chance for survival was to shout for help to the guard who had left them both in the cell.

"HELP!" Jimmy screamed at the top of his lungs.

"Jimmy, Jimmy! Wake up, Jimmy!" a familiar voice shouted. Jimmy suddenly realized that he was not in a cell, but he was in the tent, being shaken by his father.

"Jimmy! You have been having a nightmare. Wake up."

What had been a great camping trip had turned into a nightmare. But they had both learned important lessons: Pay attention to the authorities when they make an announcement and follow their instructions. Never trust that a gun is not loaded, and never shoot at a target without positive identification, even in a dream. And when your mother gives you some advice—even if it's just not to take sauerkraut on a campout and eat it before going to bed—believe her!

Story Outline

I. Jimmy and his dad, Mr. Simpson, are packing up for a weekend camping trip. Mr. Simpson ignores his wife's advice not to pack a large can of sauerkraut as part of their food provisions.

II. Mr. Simpson and Jimmy are camping in the Jacksonville State Forest when they hear a radio announcement that they should leave the area because a feared murderer, "Gold Tooth," had escaped from the local prison.

III. Jimmy wants to go home, but Mr. Simpson notes that the prisoner is heading in a different direction from them and is twenty miles away.

IV. To calm Jimmy down, Mr. Simpson pulls an unloaded gun from their gear and places it between them in the tent.

V. Jimmy wakes up hearing noises outside the tent.

VI. He sees the shadow of a man on the tent and shoots at him, striking him dead.

VII. Jimmy is thrown into a jail cell by a relative of the man he killed.

VIII. The guard returns and throws another murderer in the cell with him, who turns out to be the real Gold Tooth.

IX. Gold Tooth knows that Jimmy tried to kill him, so he goes after him and begins squeezing the life out of him.

X. Jimmy wakes from his sauerkraut-induced nightmare and realizes it has all been a dream!

XI. But Jimmy and his dad learn several lessons from this experience: Do not ignore the advice in official bulletins; never trust that a gun is empty; never shoot without identifying the target; and always pay attention to what Mom has to say!

4

BENEATH THE LONE POST

by David R. Scott

As a young boy, Brenton Fielding had always been fascinated with the lifestyles of Native Americans. Each day he would tromp through the fields near his home, combing the turned soil for arrowheads and artifacts. His room was cluttered with antique books, authentic clothing, and other relics that he found in the woods.

In his later years he became less and less interested in Indians and began his career in agriculture. He enjoyed his life on the farm and enjoyed spending time tending crops in his fields. One day, however, he found something that rekindled his love for Native Americans . . . a flint ax head. The ax still held its polished edge and became the farmer's most prized possession. He carved a beautiful handle for the blade and always carried it with him on his tractor when he worked.

One day, while reaping his autumn harvest, Brenton accidentally lost his treasured ax head. He did not continue working but instead began looking for the missing artifact. Much to his dismay, he could not find it anywhere, and he sadly returned to his home.

That night, Brenton dreamed that he was again a small boy coming home from school through the woods. Suddenly, an Indian appeared and began chasing him down the path in the direction of his home. The Indian's face was painted black, and his hair was tied in long braids down either side of his chest. Young Brenton ran faster than ever before, and with each step he could hear the Indian brave asking for his sacred ax to be returned. Brenton blasted through the front door, grabbed the ax, and, out of fear, turned and killed the Indian with a blow to the head.

In his dream Brenton dragged the Indian far out into the field so that no one would find his remains. He buried the body near a lone fence post as deeply into the ground as he possibly could.

A singe crash of thunder awakened Brenton from his nightmare. He walked over to the window and gazed though the curtain of rain sprinkling over his crops. Due to the darkness he could see hardly anything at all, yet suddenly, a great flash of lightning ignited the sky, and in that one instant the only thing he saw was the lone fence post of his nightmare.

Days went by, and then weeks. The urge to dig beneath the post was overwhelming, yet the fear of what he might find there was even greater. Winter soon set in, and along with the cold months came constant torment. All Brenton

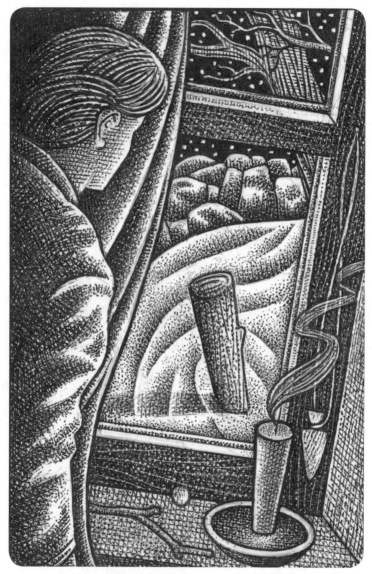

Beneath the Lone Post

could do was peer out his window at the post swirled with a beard of frosty white snow. Every day he hoped he would come across the ax head, to prove that the dream was a figment of his imagination, but it never appeared. The breakup of winter and the blooming of spring were fast upon him. Brenton had nearly forgotten about the ax, simply because he was preparing for the planting season. But while carrying a sack of seed to the barn, Brenton noticed the lone fence pole, and once more the torment returned. Running to the barn, he grabbed a spade and headed for the fence post.

Quickly he began digging into the soft muddy earth. His shovel was heavy, and sweat poured from his brow, yet his pace was rhythmically steady. The spring mud slowly began piling up around his feet, and although tired he could not bring himself to slow down. Finally he heard a click.

He cleaned the remaining mud away with his hands only to discover the missing ax head embedded deeply into a human skull. Next to the skull lay a rotting wooden handle . . . it was the handle he had carved.

Leaving the items where he found them, Brenton filled the hole and placed his best arrowhead on top of the grave. The next day the arrowhead was gone, and from that day forth Brenton never revealed the story of the lone post to anyone.

Story Outline

I. A farmer finds an ax head, which he cherishes until the day he loses it in his field while working.

II. He dreams that an Indian brave is chasing him, asking for the ax back. In the dream he kills the brave with the axe and buries them both in the field near a lone fence post.

III. Thunder awakens him from his dream, and in a lightning flash he sees a lone fence post on the property.

IV. He resists the urge to dig beneath the fence post until the following spring.

V. As he digs beside the fence post, he finds the missing ax head, deeply embedded into a human skull, with the handle that he had carved for the ax rotting next to it.

VI. He reburies the ax and skull and leaves his best arrowhead as an offering on top of the grave.

5

LOST FACE

by Jack London

This little-known story is one of Jack London's best. The surprise ending, coupled with a scary woodland setting, make it an ideal campfire story. The initial paragraphs, relating to the hero's wanderings can be condensed in the telling, and place names can be eliminated or greatly simplified by the teller.

It was the end. Subienkow had traveled a long trail of bitterness and horror, homing like a dove for the capitals of Europe, and here, farther away then ever, in Russian America, the trail ceased. He sat in the snow, arms tied behind him, awaiting the torture. He stared curiously before him at a huge Cossack, prone in the snow, moaning in his pain. The men had finished handling the giant and turned him over to the women. That they had exceeded the fiendishness of the men the man's cries attested.

Subienkow looked on and shuddered. He was not afraid to die. He had carried his life too long in his hands, on that weary trail from Warsaw to Nulato, to shudder at mere dying. But he objected to the torture. It offended his soul. And this offense, in turn, was not due to the mere pain he must endure, but to the sorry spectacle the pain would make of him. He knew that he would pray, and beg, and entreat, even as Big Ivan and the others that had gone before. This would not be nice. To pass out bravely and cleanly, with a smile and a jest—ah, that would have been the way. But to lose control, to have his soul upset by the pangs of the flesh, to screech and gibber like an ape, to become the veriest beast—ah, that was what was so terrible.

There had been no chance to escape. From the beginning, when he dreamed the fiery dream of Poland's independence, he had become a puppet in the hands of fate. From the beginning, at Warsaw, at St. Petersburg, in the Siberian mines, in Kamchatka, on the crazy boats of the fur thieves, fate had been driving him to this end.

Without doubt, in the foundations of the world was graved this end for him—for him, who was so fine and sensitive, whose nerves scarcely sheltered under his skin, who was a dreamer and a poet and an artist. Before he was dreamed of, it had been determined that the quivering bundle of sensitiveness that constituted him should be doomed to live in raw and howling savagery, and to die in this far land of night, in this dark place beyond the last boundaries of the world.

He sighed. So that thing before him was Big Ivan—
Big Ivan the giant, the man without nerves, the man of
iron, the Cossack turned freebooter of the seas, who was
as phlegmatic as an ox, with a nervous system so low that
what was pain to ordinary men was scarcely a tickle to
him. Well, well, trust these Nulato Indians to find Big
Ivan's nerves and trace them to the roots of his quivering
soul. They were certainly doing it. It was inconceivable
that a man could suffer so much and yet live. Big Ivan was
paying for his low order of nerves. Already he had lasted
twice as long as any of the others.

Subienkow felt that he could not stand the Cossack's
sufferings much longer. Why didn't Ivan die? He would
go mad if that screaming did not cease. But when it did
cease, his turn would come. And there was Yakaga awaiting him, too, grinning at him even now in anticipation—
Yakaga, whom only last week he had kicked out of the
fort, and upon whose face he had laid the last of his dog
whip. Yakaga would attend to him. Doubtlessly Yakaga
was saving for him more refined tortures, more exqui-
site nerve racking. Ah! That must have been a good one,
from the way Ivan screamed. The squaws bending over
him stepped back with laughter and clapping of hands.
Subienkow saw the monstrous thing that had been per-
petrated and began to laugh hysterically. The Indians
looked at him in wonderment that he should laugh. But
Subienkow could not stop.

This would never do. He controlled himself, the spas-
modic twitchings slowly dying away. He strove to think
of other things and began reading back in his own life.
He remembered his mother and his father, and the little

spotted pony, and the French tutor who had taught him dancing and sneaked him an old worn copy of Voltaire. Once more he saw Paris, and dreary London, and gay Vienna, and Rome. And once more he saw that wild group of youths who had dreamed, even as he, the dream of an independent Poland, with a king of Poland on the throne at Warsaw. Ah, there it was that the long trail began. Well, he had lasted longest. One by one, beginning with the two executed at St. Petersburg, he took up the count of the passing of those brave spirits. Here one had been beaten to death by a jailer, and there, on that blood-stained highway of the exiles, where they had marched for endless months, beaten and maltreated by their Cossack guards, another had dropped by the way. Always it had been savagery—brutal, bestial savagery. They had died, of fever, in the mines, under the knout. The last two had died after the escape, in the battle with the Cossacks, and he alone had won to Kamchatka with the stolen papers and the money of a traveler he had left lying in the snow.

It had been nothing but savagery. All the years, with his heart in studios and theaters and courts, he had been hemmed in by savagery. He had purchased his life with blood. Everybody had been killed. He had killed that traveler for his passports. He had proved that he was a man of parts by dueling with two Russian officers on a single day. He had had to prove himself in order to win a place among the fur thieves. He had had to win that place. Behind him lay the thousand-years-long road across all Siberia and Russia. He could not escape that way. The only way was ahead, across the dark and icy sea of Bering to Alaska. The way had led from savagery to deeper savagery.

On the scurvy-rotten ships of the fur thieves, out of food and out of water, buffeted by the interminable storms of that stormy sea, men had become animals. Thrice he had sailed east from Kamchatka. And thrice, after all manner of hardship and suffering, the survivors had come back to Kamchatka. There had been no outlet for escape, and he could not go back the way he had come, for the mines and the knout awaited him.

Again, the fourth and last time, he had sailed east. He had been with those who first found the fabled Seal Islands; but he had not returned with them to share the wealth of fur in the mad orgies of Kamchatka. He had sworn never to go back. He knew that to win to those dear capitals of Europe he must go on. So he had changed ships and remained in the dark new land. His comrades were Slavonian hunters and Russian adventurers, Mongols and Tatars, and Siberian aborigines; and through the savages of the New World they had cut a path of blood. They had massacred whole villages that refused to furnish the fur tribute; and they in turn had been massacred by ships' companies. He, with one Finn, had been the sole survivors of such a company. They had spent a winter of solitude and starvation on a lonely Aleutian isle, and their rescue in the spring by another fur ship had been one chance in a thousand.

But always the terrible savagery had hemmed him in. Passing from ship to ship, and ever refusing to return, he had come to the ship that explored the south. All down the Alaskan coast they had encountered nothing but hosts of savages. Every anchorage among the beetling islands or under the frowning cliffs of the mainland had meant a battle or a storm. Either the gales blew, threatening destruction, or the war canoes came off, manned by howling natives with the war paint on their faces, who came to learn the bloody virtues of the sea rovers' gunpowder. South, south they had coasted, clear to the myth land of California. Here, it was said, were Spanish adventurers who had fought their way up from Mexico. He had had hopes of those Spanish adventurers. Escaping to them, the rest would have been easy—a year or two, what did it matter more or less?—and he would win to Mexico, then a ship, and Europe would be his. But they had met no Spaniards. Only had they encountered the same impregnable wall of savagery. The denizens of the confines of the world, painted for war, had driven them back from the shores. At last, when one boat was cut off and every man killed, the commander had abandoned the quest and sailed back to the North.

The years had passed. He had served under Tebenkoff when Michaelovski Redoubt was built. He had spent two years in the Kuskokwim country. Two summers, in the month of June, he had managed to be at the head of Kotzebue Sound. Here, at this time, the tribes assembled for barter; here were to be found spotted deerskins from Siberia, ivory from the Diomedes, walrus skins from the shores of the Arctic, strange stone lamps, passing in trade from tribe to tribe, no one knew whence, and once, a hunting knife of English make; and here, Subienkow knew, was the school in which to learn geography. For he met Eskimos from Norton Sound, from King Island and St. Lawrence Island, from Cape Prince of Wales, and Point Barrow. Such places had other names, and their distances were measured in days.

It was a vast region these trading savages came from, and a vaster region from which, by repeated trade, their stone lamps and that steel knife had come. Subienkow bullied and cajoled and bribed. Every far journeyer or strange tribesman was brought before him. Perils unaccountable and unthinkable were mentioned, as well as wild beasts, hostile tribes, impenetrable forests, and mighty mountain ranges; but always from beyond came the rumor and the tale of white-skinned men, blue of eye and fair of hair, who fought like devils and who sought always for furs. They were to the east—far, far to the east. No one had seen them. It was the word that had been passed along.

It was a hard school. One could not learn geography very well through the medium of strange dialects, from dark minds that mingled fact and fable and that measured distances by "sleeps" that varied according to the difficulty of the going. But at last came the whisper that gave Subienkow courage. In the east lay a great river where were these blue-eyed men. The river was called the Yukon. South of Michaelovski Redoubt emptied another great river which the Russians knew as the Kwikpak. These two rivers were one, ran the whisper.

Subienkow returned to Michaelovski. For a year he urged an expedition up the Kwikpak. Then arose Malakoff, the Russian half-breed, to lead the wildest and most ferocious of the hell's broth of mongrel adventurers who had crossed from Kamchatka. Subienkow was his lieutenant. They threaded the mazes of the great delta of the Kwikpak, picked up the first low hills on the northern bank, and for half a thousand miles, in skin canoes loaded to the gunwales with trade goods and ammunition, fought their way against the five-knot current of a river that ran from two to ten miles wide in a channel many fathoms deep. Malakoff decided to build the fort at Nulato. Subienkow urged to go farther. But he quickly reconciled himself to Nulato. The long winter was coming on. It would be better to wait. Early the following summer, when the ice was gone, he would disappear up the Kwikpak and work his way to the Hudson's Bay Company's posts. Malakoff had never heard the whisper that the Kwikpak was the Yukon, and Subienkow did not tell him.

Came the building of the fort. It was enforced labor. The tiered walls of logs arose to the sighs and groans of the Nulato Indians. The lash was laid upon their backs, and it was the iron hand of the freebooters of the sea that laid on the lash. There were Indians who ran away, and when they were caught they were brought back and spread-eagled before the fort, where they and their tribe learned the efficacy of the knout. Two died under it; others were injured for life; and the rest took the lesson to heart and ran away no more. The snow was flying ere the fort was finished, and then it was the time for furs. A heavy tribute was laid upon the tribe. Blows and lashings continued, and that the tribute should be paid, the women and children were held as hostages and treated with the barbarity that only the fur thieves knew.

Well, it had been a sowing of blood, and now was come the harvest. The fort was gone. In the light of its burning, half the fur thieves had been cut down. The other half had passed under the torture. Only Subienkow remained, or Subienkow and Big Ivan, if that whimpering, moaning thing in the snow could be called Big Ivan.

Subienkow caught Yakaga grinning at him. There was no gainsaying Yakaga. The mark of the lash was still on his face. After all, Subienkow could not blame him, but he disliked the thought of what Yakaga would do to him. He thought of appealing to Makamuk, the head chief; but his judgment told him that such appeal was useless. Then, too, he thought of bursting his bonds and dying fighting. Such an end would be quick. But he could not break his bonds. Caribou thongs were stronger than he. Still devising, another thought came to him. He signed for Makamuk, and that an interpreter who knew the coast dialect should be brought.

"Oh, Makamuk," he said, "I am not minded to die, I am a great man, and it were foolishness for me to die. In truth, I shall not die. I am not like these other carrion."

He looked at the moaning thing that had once been Big Ivan and stirred it contemptuously with his toe.

"I am too wise to die. Behold, I have a great medicine. I alone know this medicine. Since I am not going to die, I shall exchange this medicine with you."

"What is this medicine?" Makamuk demanded.

"It is a strange medicine."

Subienkow debated with himself for a moment, as if loath to part with the secret.

"I will tell you. A little bit of this medicine rubbed on the skin makes the skin hard like a rock, hard like iron, so that no cutting weapon can cut it. The strongest blow of a cutting weapon is a vain thing against it. A bone knife becomes like a piece of mud; and it will turn the edge of the iron knives we have brought among you. What will you give me for the secret of the medicine?"

"I will give you your life," Makamuk made answer through the interpreter.

Subienkow laughed scornfully.

"And you shall be a slave in my house until you die."

The Pole laughed more scornfully.

"Untie my hands and feet and let us talk," he said.

The chief made the sign; and when he was loosed Subienkow rolled a cigarette and lighted it.

"This is foolish talk," said Makamuk. "There is no such medicine. It cannot be. A cutting edge is stronger than any medicine."

The chief was incredulous, and yet he wavered. He had seen too many deviltries of fur thieves that worked. He could not wholly doubt.

"I will give you your life; but you shall not be a slave," he announced.

"More than that."

Subienkow played his game as coolly as if he were bartering for a fox skin.

"It is a very great medicine. It has saved my life many times. I want a sled and dogs, and six of your hunters to travel with me down the river and give me safety to one day's sleep from Michaelovski Redoubt."

"You must live here and teach us all of your deviltries," was the reply.

Subienkow shrugged his shoulders and remained silent. He blew cigarette smoke out on the icy air, and curiously regarded what remained of the big Cossack.

"That scar!" Makamuk said suddenly, pointing to the Pole's neck, where a livid mark advertised the slash of a knife in a Kamchatkan brawl. "The medicine is not good. The cutting edge was stronger than the medicine."

"It was a strong man that drove the stroke." (Subienkow considered.)

"Stronger than you, stronger than your strongest hunter, stronger than he."

Again, with the toe of his moccasin, he touched the Cossack—a grisly spectacle, no longer conscious—yet in whose dismembered body the pain-racked life clung and was loath to go.

"Also the medicine was weak. For at that place there were no berries of a certain kind, of which I see you have plenty in this country. The medicine here will be strong."

"I will let you go downriver," said Makamuk, "and the sled and the dogs and the six hunters to give you safety shall be yours."

"You are slow," was the cool rejoinder. "You have committed an offense against my medicine in that you did not at once accept my terms. Behold, I now demand more. I want one hundred beaver skins." (Makamuk sneered.) "I want one hundred pounds of dried fish." (Makamuk nodded, for fish were plentiful and cheap.) "I want two sleds—one for me and one for my furs and fish. And my rifle must be returned to me. If you do not like the price, in a little while the price will grow."

Yakaga whispered to the chief.

"But how can I know your medicine is true medicine?" Makamuk asked.

"It is very easy. First, I shall go into the woods—"

Again Yakaga whispered to Makamuk, who made a suspicious dissent.

"You can send twenty hunters with me," Subienkow went on. "You see, I must get the berries and the roots with which to make the medicine. Then, when you have brought the two sleds and loaded on them the fish and the beaver skins and the rifle, and when you have told of the six hunters who will go with me—then, when all is ready, I will rub the medicine on my neck, so, and lay my neck there on that log. Then can your strongest hunter take the ax and strike three times on my neck. You yourself can strike the first three times."

Makamuk stood with gaping mouth, drinking in this latest and most wonderful magic of the fur thieves.

"But first," the Pole added hastily, "between each blow I must put on fresh medicine. The ax is heavy and sharp, and I want no mistakes."

"All that you have asked shall be yours," Makamuk cried in a rush of acceptance. "Proceed to make your medicine."

Subienkow concealed his elation. He was playing a desperate game, and there must be no slips. He spoke arrogantly.

"You have been slow. My medicine is offended. To make the offense clean you must give me your daughter."

He pointed to the girl, an unwholesome creature, with a cast in one eye and a bristling wolf tooth. Makamuk was angry, but the Pole remained imperturbable, rolling and lighting another cigarette.

"Make haste," he threatened. "If you are not quick, I shall demand yet more."

In the silence that followed, the dreary Northland scene faded from before him, and he saw once more his native land, and France, and once, as he glanced at the wolf-toothed girl, he remembered another girl, a singer and a dancer, whom he had known when first as a youth he came to Paris.

"What do you want with the girl?" Makamuk asked.

"To go down the river with me." Subienkow glanced her over critically. "She will make a good wife, and it is an honor worthy of my medicine to be married to your blood."

Again he remembered the singer and dancer and hummed aloud a song she had taught him. He lived the old life over, but in a detached, impersonal sort of way, looking at the memory pictures of his own life as if they were pictures in a book of anybody's life. The chief's voice, abruptly breaking the silence, startled him.

"It shall be done," said Makamuk. "The girl shall go down the river with you. But be it understood that I myself strike the three blows with the ax on your neck."

"But each time I shall put on the medicine," Subienkow answered, with a show of ill-concealed anxiety.

"You shall put the medicine on between each blow. Here are the hunters who shall see you do not escape. Go into the forest and gather your medicine."

Makamuk had been convinced of the worth of the medicine by the Pole's rapacity. Surely nothing less than the greatest of medicines could enable a man in the shadow of death to stand up and drive an old woman's bargain.

"Besides," whispered Yakaga, when the Pole, with this guard, had disappeared among the spruce trees, "when you have learned the medicine you can easily destroy him."

"But how can I destroy him?" Makamuk argued. "His medicine will not let me destroy him."

"There will be some part where he has not rubbed the medicine," was Yakaga's reply. "We will destroy him through that part. It may be his ears. Very well; we will thrust a spear in one ear and out the other. Or it may be his eyes. Surely the medicine will be much too strong to rub on his eyes."

The chief nodded. "You are wise, Yakaga. If he possesses no other devil things, we will then destroy him."

Subienkow did not waste time in gathering the ingredients for his medicine. He selected whatsoever came to hand such as spruce needles, the inner bark of the willow, a strip of birch bark, and a quantity of mossberries, which he made the hunters dig up for him from beneath the snow. A few frozen roots completed his supply, and he led the way back to camp.

Makamuk and Yakaga crouched beside him, noting the quantities and kinds of the ingredients he dropped into the pot of boiling water.

"You must be careful that the mossberries go in first," he explained. "And—of yes, one other thing—the finger of a man. Here, Yakaga, let me cut off your finger."

But Yakaga put his hands behind him and scowled.

"Just a small finger," Subienkow pleaded.

"Yakaga, give him your finger," Makamuk commanded.

"There be plenty of fingers lying around," Yakaga grunted, indicating the human wreckage in the snow of the score of persons who had been tortured to death.

"It must be the finger of a live man," the Pole objected.

"Then shall you have the finger of a live man." Yakaga strode over to the Cossack and sliced off a finger.

"He is not yet dead," he announced, flinging the bloody trophy in the snow at the Pole's feet, "Also, it is a good finger, because it is large."

Subienkow dropped it into the fire under the pot and began to sing. It was a French love song that with great solemnity he sang into the brew.

"Without these words I utter into it the medicine is worthless," he explained. "The words are the chiefest strength of it. Behold, it is ready."

"Name the words slowly, that I may know them," Makamuk commanded.

"Not until after the test. When the ax flies back three times from my neck, then will I give you the secret of the words."

"But if the medicine is not good medicine?" Makamuk queried anxiously.

Subienkow turned upon him wrathfully. "My medicine is always good. However, if it is not good, then do by me as you have done to the others. Cut me up a bit at a time, even as you have cut him up." He pointed to Cossack. "The medicine is now cool. Thus I rub it on my neck, saying this further medicine."

With great gravity he slowly intoned a line of the "Marseillaise," at the same time rubbing the villainous brew thoroughly into his neck.

An outcry interrupted his play acting. The giant Cossack, with a last resurgence of his tremendous vitality, had arisen to his knees. Laughter and cries of surprise and applause arose from the Nulatos, as Big Ivan began flinging himself about in the snow with mighty spasms.

Subienkow was made sick by the sight, but he mastered his qualms and made believe to be angry.

"This will not do," he said. "Finish him, and then we will make the test. Here, you, Yakaga, see that his noise ceases."

While this was being done, Subienkow turned to Makamuk. "And remember, you are to strike hard. This is not baby work. Here, take the ax and strike the log, so I can see you strike like a man."

Makamuk obeyed, striking twice, precisely and with vigor, cutting out a large chip.

"It is well." Subienkow looked about him at the circle of savage faces that somehow seemed to symbolize the wall of savagery that had hemmed him about ever since the Czar's police had first arrested him in Warsaw. "Take your ax, Makamuk, and stand so. I shall lie down. When I raise my hand, strike, and strike with all your might. And be careful that no one stands behind you. The medicine is good, and the ax may bounce from off my neck and right out of your hands."

He looked at the two sleds, with the dogs in harness, loaded with furs and fish. His rifle lay on top of the beaver skins. The six hunters who were to act as his guard stood by the sleds.

"Where is the girl?" the Pole demanded. "Bring her up to the sleds before the test goes on."

When this had been carried out, Subienkow lay down in the snow, resting his head on the log like a tired child about to sleep. He had lived so many dreary years that he was indeed tired.

"I laugh at you and your strength, O Makamuk," he said. "Strike, and strike hard."

Lost Face

He lifted his hand. Makamuk swung the ax, a broadax for the squaring of logs. The bright steel flashed through the frosty air, poised for a perceptible instant above Makamuk's head, then descended upon Subienkow's bare neck. Clear through flesh and bone it cut its way, biting deeply into the log beneath. The amazed savages saw the head bounce a yard away from the blood-spouting trunk.

There was a great bewilderment and silence, while slowly it began to dawn in their minds that there had been no medicine. The fur thief had outwitted them. Alone, of all their prisoners, he had escaped the torture. That had been the stake for which he played. A great roar of laughter went up. Makamuk bowed his head in shame. The fur thief had fooled him. He had lost face before all his people. Still they continued to roar out their laughter. Makamuk turned, and with bowed head stalked away. He knew that thenceforth he would be no longer known as Makamuk. He would be Lost Face; the record of his shame would be with him until he died; and whenever the tribes gathered in the spring for the salmon, or in the summer for the trading, the story would pass back and forth across the campfires of how the fur thief died peaceably, at a single stroke, by the hand of Lost Face.

"Who was Lost Face?" he could hear, in anticipation, some insolent young buck demand. "Oh, Lost Face," would be the answer, "he who once was Makamuk in the days before he cut off the fur thief's head."

Story Outline

I. Subienkow is a Polish adventurer who had escaped from Poland across Siberia after an attempt at independence had been crushed by the Russian Czar. He hopes to reach Europe by way of the rugged and unexplored North American wilderness, possibly by contacting the fur traders of Hudson's Bay Company.

II. To get to Alaska he fights his way across Siberia and joins fur thieves who are looting the Indians. Subienkow attempts to learn geography from the natives, hoping to eventually escape to a more civilized area.

III. A new leader arises, Malakoff, who leads the band of fur thieves deeper into the wilderness, eventually forcing the Indians into slave labor to build a fort. The Indians who try to escape are brutally punished.

IV. The women and children are held captive, forcing the Indians to hunt and trap fur for the thieves. But the Indians revolt, burning the fort and killing the surviving fur thieves by slowly torturing them to death.

V. Subienkow has to watch as they kill Big Ivan. He is being held to the last because he lashed the face of Yakaga, an Indian who is ready for revenge. Subienkow does not mind dying, but he hates the thought that the Indians will reduce him to a whimpering pile of flesh.

VI. Subienkow tells Makamuk that he will not die because he has a powerful medicine that will prevent them from killing him. He asks the chief what he would give to learn the medicine's secret.

VII. Makamuk says he will give him his life and make him a slave the rest of his life. Subienkow is scornful. The chief then says he would not make him a slave, but Subienkow asks for more than that.

VIII. Subienkow demands that he receive a sled, dogs, and six warriors to provide him safety on his return to the base camp called Michaelovski Redoubt.

IX. Makamuk notices a scar on Subienkow's neck and says that the medicine is weak. Subienkow replies that it was a very strong person, stronger than Big Ivan, who drove that stroke, and that the medicine was weak because he lacked enough special berries at the place where the wound was made, but that there are plenty of these berries around their camp.

X. Makamuk agrees to provide the sled, dogs, and warriors, but Subienkow sneers that he was too slow in granting his demands, and that he now wants one hundred beaver skins, one hundred pounds of fish, two sleds to carry the furs and fish, and his rifle returned.

XI. Yakaga asks how they would know that the medicine is real. Subienkow explains that he will go into the woods (accompanied by twenty warriors) and pick the ingredients, then when ready he will smear it on his neck and the strongest of the Indians can take an ax and strike his neck three times.

XII. Makamuk agrees, but Subienkow says he answered too slowly, and now he demands more, he wants Makamuk's daughter. Makamuk agrees, but says that he personally will get to use the ax. Subienkow, with ill-concealed anxiety, makes the point that he must be allowed to apply more of the medicine to his neck between each of the blows.

XIII. Yakaga and the chief decide that they will kill Subienkow when they learn the secret of his medicine, as he will not cover his whole body, or if he does, they will be able to kill through an uncovered spot.

XIV. Subienkow quickly picks the ingredients. Makamuk and Yakaga watch as he mixes them together. He also needs the finger from a man and wants to cut off Yakaga's finger. (Just a small finger, he says, when Yakaga puts his hands behind his back and scowls.)

XV. Makamuk commands Yakaga to give him a finger, but Yakaga points to all of the dead bodies lying around. Subienkow says that it must come from a live person, so Yakaga cuts a finger from Big Ivan, who is still barely alive, and tosses it to Subienkow.

XVI. Subienkow rubs the medicine on his neck. When Big Ivan regains consciousness and starts flailing around in the snow, Subienkow demands that they kill Big Ivan to stop the noise. He makes Makamuk show that he can use the ax like a man, then places his head on the block.

XVII. Makamuk strikes a hard blow, cutting off Subienkow's head—and then realizes that he has been fooled. Subienkow has escaped their torture, and the chief is laughed at. He loses his position as chief and will forever be known as "Lost Face."

6

THE BOG

by Doc Forgey

This original story went through a metamor-
phosis from its first telling, which had the four
friends canoeing into a hidden valley that was
reached through a cave entrance. Originally
called "The Hidden Valley," it did not explain
how such a neat valley could remain unfound
on the maps. So I invented the bog.

Four members of Bensenville Troop 752 had been friends
all their lives. Scouting had allowed them to cement that
friendship even further on many canoeing and camping
trips near their home town and on several high-adventure
trips in Minnesota and New Mexico. But what lay ahead
of them was far more sinister than any adventure they

could have dreamed of . . . and it was going to happen practically in their own backyard.

Just outside of Bensenville there was a fairly large swamp, known locally simply as "The Bog." It was large enough to be deep and dense, but not large enough to attract attention of developers, park service personnel, or even conservationists. The bog had always been there. No roads went near it, no communities were positioned nearby—the bog sat by itself, tucked in a little-used portion of the state where time had passed it by.

The stagnant water in the bog seemed lifeless. It attracted no fishermen. There was an unusual scarcity of bird life, so no bird-watcher ventured into the hordes of mosquitoes to visit its remote water. Yet the bog seemed so dense that it was hard to imagine that there was not some living thing, even a whole slough of living things, within its borders.

Do not let me give the impression that this swamp was actually lifeless. Everyone who had ventured into the waters near its edge could vouch for the fact that indeed there was life in the swamp. The mosquitoes had neighbors—biting gnats, blackflies, swarms of bees, and although the waters seemed to produce few fish, leeches abounded.

Oh, the waters of the bog had been tested to determine if there were pollutants, radioactivity, or unusual chemicals dissolved in them. The tests had always shown nothing of interest. And so the bog continued to be abandoned.

It was abandoned for another reason beyond lack of interest: There just seemed to be something mysterious about its uncharted waters, perhaps something that might even be considered sinister. People tended to shy away from encountering the place—after all there was never a really good reason to go there anyway. Even the Indians who used to roam that area had apparently avoided the bog's confines.

But for Ralph, Bobby, David, and Chris, the bog held a special attraction. At first they paid little attention to it. They were having fun with Troop 752 just starting their camping adventures. Then those high-adventure trips consumed their interest. But with these trips behind them, their thoughts turned to "The Bog." They knew how to handle the bugs they thought. They certainly knew how to camp and canoe. The swampy ground might make pitching a tent difficult—and perhaps there would be snakes and other creatures slithering along the ground—so they decided to pack along army surplus jungle hammocks with netting, besides their two tents.

As Ralph and Bobby were slightly older than the other two, they would each take the stern of a canoe, with David and Chris manning the bow. Water filtration pumps, fire starter, hand ax and saw, as well as sleeping bags and other gear were divided equally between the two canoes—in case something happened to one of them. Each boy carried a compass. There was a topographical map of the area, but it was featureless in the vicinity of the bog, except for map symbols representing a swamp.

The boys decided that they would leave the week school was out for summer vacation. All was ready when the time came, and early one morning the four excited friends shoved off from the local highway bridge that spanned a watery section of the bog.

The wilderness opened up on all sides of them, with the air feeling heavy and smelling from the lush vegetation. They had expected mosquitoes, so they were ready with the bug dope to keep them off. What they did not expect was the maze of islands, which they were finding difficult to navigate around. Frequently the channels were choked with weeds or simply played out, ending on a marshy shore.

Bubbles of marsh gas occasionally caused a sudden splash in the water near them, which seemed to accent the eerie feeling that they were all experiencing. The boys stopped on a marshy piece of land for lunch the first day, carefully purifying their water, which they acquired by shoving down on mats of floating seaweed and thus allowing water to percolate into the depression that formed. The canoes were sluggish in their forward motion because of the drag of seaweed, which also increased difficulty in paddling.

The weather favored them the first night so that by sunset they had selected a suitable campsite, unloaded the canoes, pitched the tents, and collected and sawed a store of firewood. It was easier to prepare drinking water this time, as there was a deeper channel by the island that they had chosen for the night. They were all prepared for bad weather. The boys cooked a good supper and, as the mosquitoes were not all that bad, they sat around the campfire—happy to be in the great outdoors and on an adventure in an uncharted wilderness at that!

The strangest thing about that night was the almost total lack of wildlife. It was as if they were canoeing back into time, into some primitive swamp of the past. The

The Bog

deep stillness made many of the sounds around them seem amplified, and the boys' feeling a little keyed up also added to the startle each of them felt when they heard *PLOP* in the water right next to their camp. No further swishing sounds were heard, so the boys decided it was a lump of earth from the bank caving into the water.

In the night as they lay in their tents, once again they heard the swish of water.

It was barely five o'clock when daylight glowed along the eastern horizon of the bog. The two tents were capped and wreathed with smoky trails of fast-melting mist. In the open spaces the ground was drenched with dew. Ralph lit the fire so that an hour later, when the others got up, hot water would be ready and a bed of coals formed to make cooking breakfast less of a chore. He set forth on an exploration of his island but had gone barely ten yards when alongside the bank a giant *WHOOSH* occurred. Ralph caught his breath at the sound, but then he soon saw what was happening. A large bubble of methane gas had escaped from the swampy floor of the bog, and it suddenly surfaced, bringing large chunks of rotten vegetation with it. A whole mat of this material floated and bobbed in the wake of the sudden gas escape.

Ralph cut his exploration of the island short and returned to the campsite. He had to wait patiently for about half an hour before the other boys got up, so he busied himself by fixing breakfast over the hot bed of coals that he had made, even though it was David's turn to be chef that day. After breakfast he told them of his discovery, about the source of the *SWOOSH* they had heard the night before.

"Well that explains these clumps of floating debris that I've been having to push out of the way of the canoe," Chris remarked.

"Yeah, and some of those clumps are so big that they seem to be pushing right back," David, the other bowman, added.

"I've heard of something like this before," Bobby mentioned. "In one of the large swamps down south, maybe it was the Everglades or the Okeefenokee, bubbles of methane gas bubble up large amounts of debris from the swamp floor. Those mats float around and act as a platform for larger plants to live on. They become floating islands. When roots from the plants become long enough, they anchor the floating islands, which become permanently fixed in one place."

Finished with breakfast, the boys were anxious to shove off before the day became too warm. The reflection of the sun on the water and the stifling thickness of the air made the work of paddling their canoes all the more difficult.

"Ralph, what will we do if these islands we are charting float around and change their positions?" Bobby called over from his canoe. "We could get stuck back in this swamp forever!"

Ralph shouted back, "I've been thinking along those lines myself."

A fairly large stretch of open water promised to be a pleasant interlude from dragging their boats through weeds and trying to pole through the muck at the bottom. As they approached the open water, they noticed that the bottom deepened, deepened beyond the reach of their paddles.

But it was not to be an easy crossing. As the boys paddled, they suddenly realized that they were not making much progress toward the opposite shore. It seemed as if they were glued to the water's surface. The light breeze was not hurting or helping them. It caused a small chop of waves, which was insignificant. It just seemed as if they struggled without progress. The breeze calmed down the insect problem, and it gave the boys a chance to yank off their shirts and the insect head nets. Ralph soon realized that they were all sweating hard with everyone paddling furiously, almost savagely along, but they were getting nowhere.

"Rats," he shouted. "Hey, let's all cool it for a while. We're not going anywhere. Let's stop for a while and see what happens."

He got no argument from the others. They stopped and rested their paddles across the canoe gunnels, stretched their aching muscles, and wiped the sweat off their faces. They grinned at each other at first, feeling good about the workout they'd just had. Feeling weary, yet so strangely excited . . . It was in the middle of that lake in the bewildering chatter and confusion of explanations, that, very silently, the ghost of something horrible slipped in and stood among them. It made all their explanations seem childish and untrue. They exchanged quick, anxious glances—glances that were questioning and expressive of the dismay that they were beginning to acknowledge. There was a sense of wonder, of poignant distress, of trepidation. Alarm stood waiting at their elbows. This ghost was a realization that something they did not understand was having its way with them.

They now rested quietly after their initial joyful excitement, feeling the little quivers that the light, choppy waves made against their canoes. But as they bobbed, their quietness was a manifestation of the fear that each of them was beginning to know. And none of them seemed to want to hear the others acknowledge this same fear. But something really did seem to have them in its grasp! It soon was becoming evident that their canoes were drifting toward the north side of the lake, almost at right angles to their original line of travel.

"Hey, if this lake wants us to go to that northern shore—well, let's just help it out a little. Let's start paddling!" With that almost cheerful statement from Ralph, everyone bent to the task of paddling out of this lake, which they were beginning to fear. Even then it seemed as if their progress was just not what it should be, that the lake held them with some invisible glue.

Even with this slow progress, the marshy shore of the north end soon came close enough to view easily from the canoes.

"Check it out," Chris remarked.

The shore seemed to be penetrated at regular intervals by streams that were flowing away from the lake. The land between these streams was marshy, so swampy that no obvious stopping place was evident.

"Our next campsite will be knee-deep in water if something better doesn't appear," Chris continued.

Small, swampy islands located along the north shore were similarly unsuitable for camping.

"We've got to find someplace not only dry enough, but where we can find firewood, or we'll be stuck with just our gas stove. I'd rather be able to build a fire around this spooky place," commented Bob.

There was ready agreement on that, so that even though the boys were capable of pitching hammocks above the swampy ground and cooking with their Peak 1 stoves, they anxiously sought a piece of real estate where they could construct a more secure campsite.

After several hours of probing the streams, searching among the islands, and drifting along the shore, the boys found what appeared to be an almost ideal site.

"Jeez, this place looks like it was constructed for a campsite. This may not turn out so bad after all," one of them blurted out enthusiastically as they unloaded the canoes and started squaring away their gear.

There was a restless feeling in camp that evening, and none of the boys wanted to leave the protection of the campfire. It was as if something was alive out there, something moving—slowly, almost unperceived—but yet most assuredly moving about them. The very land seemed alive. The boys felt as if there were other people out there with them.

That night they were sure of it.

The swirling and sucking sound of the water washing along the shore, as well as the feeling of dread that they all seemed to have, caused the boys to gather as much firewood as possible and maintain their fire late into the night. The eerie night noises prompted them to peer out now and again into the black void of the night. Suddenly Chris saw something! It was a campfire flickering on an island about a mile away. Someone must be there! They all looked and watched as the small campfire burned down too low for them to see any more. After it disappeared, they all watched carefully for some sign of life, but they neither saw nor heard anything the rest of the night.

The mystery of that night deepened the next day when they decided to leave their camp set up but canoe over to the island where they thought they had seen the fire. There was a long, oval-shaped island, with large bushes in the center and several clearings, but no evidence of a fire. They spent the day searching other likely spots, but they could not find any evidence of the people whose fire they saw the night before.

The next night they again kept vigil by the fire. Sure enough, at about the witching hour of midnight, they again saw the fire flicker into life. As they watched, they thought they could see people moving around the fire. It was just too far away to tell for sure. Although there was surely more of the bog to explore, this seemed to be the crux of the mystery—to find out if a lost race of people was living back there.

The next day they again canoed over to the island where they had seen the campfire. They still could see no evidence of the campsite or indication of where the fire might have been built. Chris designed a plan to solve the mystery. He decided that it would be a good idea for them to move to the island and camp out there instead of staying where they were. But their present spot was so ideal that the others would not agree. They would have to cut firewood and canoe it over to the new site, the island seemed too damp, the clearings were small, and the bushes probably had too many mosquitoes. They all had reasons why they would not camp there, all that is except Chris.

When he could not get the others to agree to spend the night there, Chris announced he would do it by himself.

"You've got to be crazy, Chris," Bobby, his canoeing partner, told him. But Chris was determined to solve the mystery.

"And besides you guys, the camp is only about a mile away. We can shout back and forth if we need to. I'll keep my fire burning all night if I'm scared, and one of you do the same. It won't be that bad."

But the others were buying none of it. They did not want anything to do with the swampy, mysterious island. They spent the rest of the day breaking out Chris's camping gear from the rest of theirs and gathering the firewood, food, and purified water that he would need. By nightfall they had him in his camp, and they were back at theirs. As darkness fell, the fires burned brightly in both camps.

Occasionally the boys shouted across the water to each other, Chris's voice sounding so alone and far away. At just about midnight, Bobby was poking the fire with a stick, watching the sparks leap skyward. He looked up just in time to see Chris's campfire suddenly disappear! He thought, "Boy, is he a brave one. I'd probably keep my fire going all night."

Thinking to reassure Chris a little, he called over, "Hey, Chris! Did the boogeyman get you?"

But there was no reply. Bobby shouted several more times, with the other guys also joining in. But they were to receive no answer from Chris's camp that night.

At first light the next day, the three anxious boys hopped into the canoe and paddled over to Chris's campsite. His canoe was floating free, not nestled up against the shoreline where Chris's camp should have been. When I say "should have been," I mean precisely that. The boys felt a sense of panic and sickness in the pits of their stomachs when they could find no trace of Chris's camp whatsoever.

"It's just like the fires we have been seeing the previous two nights," David remarked. "There is not a sign anyone has ever been here since the beginning of time."

The boys widened their search, checking nearby islands and the shoreline, but they could find no trace of Chris. Because they had his canoe, they knew that he did not canoe away. Their great adventure had suddenly turned into a horrible nightmare.

Late in the afternoon, after checking all the surrounding areas several times, even desperately calling his name during moments of panic and anger, the boys returned with the two canoes to their campsite.

They sat around their camp in a state of shock and disbelief, discussing what they should do. They felt the overwhelming urge to travel back to town and request help. But they did not want to leave Chris by himself, wherever he was. There was a remote chance that they could still solve the mystery of the island.

Before dark Bobby came to a decision. He announced to the other guys that he was going to spend the night at Chris's island to see if he could solve the mystery. Ralph and David objected, but Bobby would not give in.

"I owe it to Chris to see if I can find out what happened to him."

Bobby packed up his gear, taking his sleeping bag, his clothes, and materials for starting a fire. He took his canoe and paddled over to the island as the others watched. Both camps started a fire just before dark. That night a thin layer of fog caused the fire from Bobby's camp to glow peculiarly in the distance. Neither Ralph nor David were about to try to sleep. They watched Bobby's camp intently as the night wore on. They called back and forth, but the distance was too great to clearly hear what was being said. Then about midnight, the very thing that Ralph and David were dreading happened again. The light from the other camp suddenly went out! They were almost in a panic, but they could do nothing about it. They knew that canoeing in the pitch-black would be hazardous. And they were too scared to consider leaving their camp. They could feel the blackness of the night crawl closer around them. The water gurgled and swished at the shoreline. The chill of the night and the surrounding dampness made the night unbearable.

The first crack of dawn found them madly paddling their canoe over to Bobby's island. But his campsite was not to be found! There was no evidence of fire, and there was no sign of Bobby's clothing, sleeping bag, or foot-prints. Nothing showing human habitation was left on the island.

The boys stood on the swampy island in a state of shock. They hardly knew what to do. Ralph wanted to go home, but David knew that he had to find the answer to this mystery and was not about to leave his friends behind. He would not listen to Ralph's pleas that they get out of there as fast as they could paddle. David sighted a gleam in the water that turned out to be Chris and Bobby's canoe floating full of water. Both life jackets and one paddle were missing.

Back at their campsite Ralph and David talked it over. "How can we possibly go back now? We may never find this place exactly again. You know how these islands seem to be floating around. We may never come to this exact point on the lakeshore or find the island that Chris and Bobby were camping on. And how about the mysterious campfires that we saw before they disappeared? If someone is out here, we must make contact with them. We can't tell their parents that we left them behind." And with that David completed their discussion. Except for one more thing. "Ralph, I know of only one way to solve this problem. We have to camp out on the island ourselves." Ralph would hear none of it. He was not about to stay on that island. "Well, Ralph," David said. "I'm going to take that canoe and go over there myself, tonight. I'm going to find out for myself what's going on."

Ralph could not believe his ears. He was not about to spend the night on that island. The campsite they had was spooky enough. And now he would have to be there alone. But he was not going to the island!

They spent that day in brooding silence. Ralph was too mad at David to really talk to him much. That night David departed and set up his camp at the island. The night seemed to fall all too quickly for Ralph, and he was glad he had a good fire to hold back the edge of darkness that surrounded his camp. There in the distance was the flicker of David's campfire.

Then, almost precisely at midnight, the very thing that Ralph was dreading the most happened. The small flickering fire on the island disappeared. Ralph's heart was in his throat it seemed. He felt a sense of panic, for he knew that he was in this swamp all alone. But more than that, he felt an incredible loneliness. The best friends he had in the world were no longer with him. And there was not a thing he could do about it.

With daybreak Ralph canoed the lonely stretch to the island. Again he found nothing. He looked carefully to see if he was on the right island. Somehow it did not look quite right. He had tramped over the marshy area so much that he had begun to know it—or so he thought. Its oblong shape seemed smaller to him. But there was no other island close enough that he could be mistaken about the location. It had been in sight from the campsite, and he had followed the same azimuth to reach it—a straight shot from the camp.

Ralph knew he really could do nothing for his friends, but he was also worried about how to get himself out of this mess. *It should not be all that hard to do,* he thought. But this time he would have to do it alone. Still he could not tear down his camp and leave just yet. He would spend one more night at their campsite, still hoping that he might be able to make some sense of his friends' disappearance.

That night he watched over the dark lake, with both fear and sadness as competing emotions. As he sat contemplating the events of the last several days, Ralph was suddenly jarred into action by what he saw in the distance. A flicker of light appeared from the island campsite! He yelled out as loud as he could, but each time he listened afterward, he heard only the swish of water in return. Soon the light again disappeared, but Ralph felt a sense of hope.

In the daylight his position did not seem so bleak. And as he gained his courage, he also resolved to do the very thing he knew all along deep down inside of himself he had to do. He would have to move his camp to that dreaded island. He would have to find out for himself what the mystery of that place was. He would not leave his friends behind, no matter what their fate—or no matter what his might become.

He broke camp early that afternoon and returned to the island. The ground in the middle of the island was spongy, but he was able to clear an area for a safe fire. He erected his tent. *Standing around here is like standing on a waterbed,* he thought to himself, as he squared his campsite away. It was sure a let down from the comfortable camp where he had spent most of the previous week.

The wetness of the place made the camp miserable. Ralph decided to place his bedding and most of his gear in the canoe and tie the canoe to the shore, allowing it to float free. As darkness fell, he made sure he had plenty of firewood on hand, some of which he had brought over from the other campsite. In fact he had about three times as much firewood as he thought he would need, certainly more than the others had brought.

With nightfall the dampness became even more noticeable. Hour followed hour as Ralph stood around the eerie camp. Suddenly he heard a familiar sound: the *SWOOSH* of water as gas from the swamp's floor bubbled up to the surface. And although this attracted his attention, not too far away near the shore, he saw a flare of light upon the water's surface. He stared at it flickering, then climbed into his canoe for a better view, allowing the canoe to drift a little way from the island's edge. Suddenly there was a massive shift of the island, the entire center where his camp was located folding in on itself, his campfire disappearing in the rush of water and hiss of steam. A wave rocked his canoe as Ralph stared in disbelief. But now he knew the secret of the island.

The campfires they had been seeing were actually will-o'-the-wisp, the phosphorescent light sometimes seen in the air over marshy places. And the island was a floating island, just as they had all known. But what they did not realize was that this floating island was not able to support their weight for a long period of time. The center of the island would suddenly sink under the weight of the campers standing on it, just folding together and dragging the struggling victims underwater. With each collapse the island had grown smaller. And Ralph realized that his companions would be buried forever beneath the muck, quicksand, and water of the lake.

Story Outline

I. Four members of Bensenville Troop 752 have been friends all their lives and are looking forward to further high adventures in the mysterious bog that lay outside of town.

II. Ralph, Bobby, David, and Chris leave the week school is out to explore the bog by canoe.

III. They find the marsh a strange place, with bubbles of marsh grass and mats of floating vegetation. The water and weeds seem to slow their progress.

IV. As they camp the first night, they hear strange plopping and swirling sounds in the water. Ralph later sees a large bubble of marsh gas come to the surface, thus explaining the sounds of the night.

V. They enter a large stretch of open water, but still find the paddling difficult. Drifting, they find they are drawn to the north shore of the lake, where they find a good dry campsite after much searching.

VI. That night they build a large fire to ward off their fears. During the night Chris sees another campfire in the distance.

VII. The boys search for the fire the next day, but they do not find it. The next night they again spot the fire. Chris decides to spend the night on an island where they think the fire may be coming from to investigate the mystery.

VIII. The boys watch Chris's campfire that night, when suddenly it goes out. They shout over to him, but they receive no reply.

IX. The next day at daybreak they canoe to his island, but they can find no trace of his camp. They find his canoe floating nearby. They search everywhere for Chris but cannot find him.

X. Against the other boys' advice, Bobby decides he will also camp out on the island. They watch his campfire that night through a thin layer of fog, until it also suddenly goes out at about midnight.

XI. The next day at daybreak Ralph and David canoe over, but again there is no trace of the campsite on the island.

XII. David realizes that they cannot go back without solving the mystery. He ignores Ralph's pleas to leave and prepares to spend the night on the island.

XIII. Ralph watches intently that night, when almost precisely at midnight David's flickering fire disappears.

XIV. Ralph finds no trace of David or his canoe the next day. He spends the day searching and decides to spend one more night at the camp, hoping to learn something about his friends' disappearances.

XV. That night as he watches over the dark lake, he sees a flicker of light from an island campfire appear again. No one answers his shouts.

XVI. He breaks camp the next day determined to solve the mystery of the island by himself.

XVII. He moves extra firewood to the boggy island and makes his camp. He leaves his canoe floating but tied to the shore.

XVIII. During the night he suddenly sees a fire nearby. He gets into his canoe to view it better and realizes that they have been looking at a methane swamp gas flare, a will-o'-the-wisp.

XIX. As Ralph watches the flare, the island collapses, folding in the middle from the weight of the firewood. He realizes that his friends, standing in the camp in the middle of the floating island, made it collapse, causing them to be sucked into the muck, quicksand, and water below.

7

THE WALKING STICK

by Doc Forgey

Have you ever had one of those days, especially when you are hiking or climbing, when you just do not have the zip and vigor that everyone else has? On one such an occasion, I decided that perhaps I was just contending with an evil spell, for I certainly could not be that much older or in that much worse shape than the rest of my party. That got me started thinking about a possible source of an evil spell for a nephew who just could not leave his uncle's things alone.

Mike had a walking stick that used to be his uncle's. He always wanted to take it camping. Hiking with it now, with the rest of the kids envious of his stick, was something he was enjoying, sort of. Sort of? Well, Mike couldn't really enjoy this moment as much as he wished. You see, the stick didn't belong to him . . . yet. It was still his uncle's, and he had been warned to leave it alone. But there it was in his grandpa's house, down in a closet filled with things—all still owned by his uncle.

But that stick. It was special and stood out from the rest of the items—even his uncle's military uniform, the one with the medals. You see his uncle had always made it clear to Mike to stay away from that stick. He wasn't to touch it, play with it, even take it out of the closet—and here he was taking it on a camping trip with the other boys in the Scout troop, just as if it were his.

He never understood why he wasn't to play with it. His uncle had never told him. In fact he had always scolded Mike for coming near it or for even asking questions about it. His uncle had been in Vietnam for many years, and there were many things that he said that Mike knew he would never understand fully. This stick was obviously part of the stuff he had brought home from that war. Mike felt that there was something sinister about it, something evil. It didn't look like much—just a stiff, light, and straight pole. But the color was black. It came to a sharp point and broadened as it went up to the top, where it formed a smooth, flat head.

The stick would have been just right for his uncle to use as a walking stick, but it was a little tall for Mike. Still, it fit well enough in his hand as they scrambled over the rough ground. Mike was always having to hurry a little to keep up with the bigger guys. The sun was becoming a little hot; the ground was uneven at times, with logs and stones covering the trail here and there; and now insects were becoming bothersome—especially in this heat. It seemed that the insects were bothering him more than the other guys. Maybe he was sweating more. As he looked at the boy ahead of him, he could tell that Jim looked comfortable. His friend was walking along the trail in an almost carefree manner. Jim had not soaked through his shirt, but Mike had. The heat was clouding his vision, hurting his brain, even bothering his hearing.

The trip became even harder as the trail led up the hill to a fire tower. A natural spring had been tapped with a faucet, providing water for the little campground about three hundred feet beneath the hilltop. As they reached the campsite, the other kids wanted to run on ahead to scramble up the tower. Mike was too exhausted to even consider climbing that last three hundred feet of hill. He flopped to his back at the last remaining tent site, breathing heavily in the stifling hot air of that summer afternoon.

The sounds of the kids in his troop faded away, up the hill. The drone of the insects seemed louder and muffled the happy sounds coming from his friends. He swatted at them aimlessly, too tired to open his eyes. The hot sun made the vegetation smell musty and strong. The babble of voices seemed to continue in the background. As he lay exhausted against his pack, Mike hoped he would never have to move again. Clutching the walking stick, which he laid along his side, he became more aware of the strong smells of the forest. Now he was even less aware of the incoherent chatter in the background, coming from the hill above him.

The Walking Stick

He paid no attention, that is, until suddenly it dawned on him that there was something different about those voices. He could not understand even an occasional word. The voices were making choppy, peculiar sounds. The insects were competing with their swarming and buzzing. Strange that his friends did not seem to notice this horrible weather, these horrible bugs. What were they doing anyway? He no longer heard the occasional sound of his scoutmaster's voice.

Mike lazily opened his eyes. What he saw shocked him wide awake. The trees had changed! The weeds, the bushes, the forest—they all had changed! Just the heat was there . . . and those mosquitoes. And the voices from above him on the hill.

But the voices were different. Mike wasn't sure what he noticed first: the fact that he could see no other camping gear around him, that he was in a thick jungle of vegetation, or that the voices he heard were not those of his friends!

His first impulse was to call out, to yell his head off for help! But there was something scary about those voices. They were excited, shouting to each other, crashing through the thick brush above him. He could tell that the people making the noises were thrashing the brush as they walked along through it, as if they were in a straight line beating the bushes, trying to flush something, or someone, out!

He thought that the voices were sinister, gruff. He realized that he should take no chances with these people. He must hide. He hated leaving his spot, because he was afraid that he would only get helplessly lost. Yet he feared for his life.

Still clutching the walking stick, Mike slid down the hill under the cover of a layer of large-leafed plants. The dirt from the forest floor stuck to his sweaty legs and clothing; the stick was slick in his sweaty hands. His movement must have attracted attention on the hill above him, for there was a commotion—the people all seemed to be coming, crashing down the hill directly toward him!

The jungle floor was steep, steep like the jungle-covered hills in Vietnam must have been where his uncle had served during the war. Mike was able to slide faster and faster, and he desperately tried to get away from the people streaming down the hill above him. As he looked up he could see them coming closer and closer. He could make out the peculiar helmets, the red star on their helmets, their rifles.

The bushes whipped him as he slid down the hill toward a stream that he could hear below. The willow-like wands of brush were cutting at his face, arms, and legs. It didn't matter. Just as long as he could get away! A bush with bright orange flowers and long spike-like thorns struck him, leaving a large thorn stuck in his right arm.

Suddenly, as he slid toward a large tree—*CRACK!* The walking stick slammed against the tree and was torn from his grasp! He suddenly plunged off a small gully— *SPLASH*—into a stream of cold water!

With a shock he looked around. The forest was hardwood, he was not in the jungle anymore. The voices from above him were those of his friends, who were excitedly climbing down the hill after him, looking for him! Mike realized that the walking stick was not in his hands any longer. The weather was pleasant and cool. The bugs were gone.

Mike could never explain to his scoutmaster or his friends what had happened to him. And he could not find the walking stick, no matter how hard he looked.

His mom took him to the doctor when he got home to have a large, strange thorn taken out of his arm. But what was really strange was that his uncle was never seen or heard from again. All traces of him vanished—and Mike wondered if his uncle could have taken his place, deep in some mysterious jungle in Vietnam! He would never know.

Story Outline

I. Mike takes his uncle's walking stick, a souvenir of the Vietnam War, with him on a hike with his Scout troop—even though he has been warned to leave it alone.

II. The troop is hiking in a forest up a hill to a fire tower.

III. While everyone else is enjoying the hike, Mike feels hotter and hotter—and is bothered by the bugs.

IV. When the troop reaches the campsite, Mike is too tired to scramble farther to the tower with the other kids. As he rests, he is surrounded by bugs and the heat.

V. Mike becomes aware that the voices of his friends have changed; the vegetation has changed—he appears to be lost in a jungle.

VI. He tries to get away from the people, probably Viet Cong, who are chasing him. As he crashes downhill toward a stream, he hits a tree and has the stick knocked away from him.

VII. After this crash, he realizes that he is back with his friends in normal woods.

VIII. The stick is lost. His mother takes him to the doctor to have a strange thorn removed from his arm. And his uncle disappears, never to be seen again.

8

THE INDIAN HEAD

by Pat Sherwood

This original story by Pat Sherwood starts with a fabricated explanation of the source of the story, a technique used to establish credibility. The "credibility factor" has a profound impact in setting the proper mood, which increases the dramatic effect of a story.

Obviously his introduction should be changed to a more personalized source by the individual storyteller, unless the kids would feel that the narrator also had camped in the high timber area of Washington State.

This story was passed on to me while on a camping trip high up in timberline in Washington State. An old-timer had wandered into our camp late one afternoon, and according to custom was asked to share our camp for dinner and a night's rest.

After supper we sat around the campfire finishing the last of the coffee. It was one of those cool, breezy evenings that always stays in your mind—dark, with just enough of a chill to turn up a collar and be thankful for the warmth and glow of the fire.

I remember looking across at the stranger who now shared our camp. He sat smoking a pipe, the whirls of smoke encircling his head, the light of the fire reflecting the whiteness of his beard, magnifying the lines that were cut deep into his face by constant exposure to the mountain winds. His eyes were clear and lively and seemed too young for the face they served. The old-timer's name has long since slipped from my memory, but I remember his face and the low, soft voice that spoke the slang of the woods well.

As the night grew darker, the conversation naturally turned to those things that go bump in the night. And on hearing that I was from Indiana, the stranger seemed to give an ear to some old voices in his memory. He then related this story, which has stayed in my mind for many years. As I sat there listening to his tale after a few moments, the past came to life again in the changing embers of the fire.

In the early 1820s there was a small trading post nestled on a river bend in the southern part of Indiana, no more than a three-day canoe trip north of Fort Vincennes. It has been said that George Rogers Clark may have passed through there on his way to defeat Hamilton at Vincennes.

The trading post was used by French trappers for many years before the revolution opened it up for the Americans. One of the Americans was a mountain of a man by the name of John Walker, "Big John" as the other trappers called him.

No one seemed to know just where John came from, and those who knew of him, knew better than to ask. It was said that he was as big as a tree, as broad and strong as any horse on the river, meaner than a badger, and as stubborn as they came. They said you had a better chance of convincing a mule he had his ears on backward than to get Big John to change his mind or give in. About the only friend John had at the post was a fur buyer by the name of Austin Handley, and their friendship, at best, was limited to conversation over a shared bottle of whiskey.

John never stayed at the trading post long, preferring to be by himself and running his traps. When he was at the post, everyone gave him a lot of ground. Being simple of mind he'd cut your heart out for the fun of it. Even the Indians would give Big John a wide berth; they thought him crazy and bad medicine. But when it came to trapping furs, the other trappers all agreed, John was the best. He would stay out longer and trap the toughest of terrain, and when he did come to the trading post, he'd have the largest and most pelts of any trapper in the area.

This was the only thing that seemed important to John, finding the largest and best of pelts. He was always on the lookout for better areas to trap and bigger furs to take. Simple as he was, one thing stayed ever in his mind, that the local Indians always seemed to have larger and thicker furs than he did.

So Big John set out to find the elusive trapping ground that the local Indians kept so secret. His search took him all over the surrounding forest, through thick swamps, and over what seemed like every hollow in the territory. Finally John happened to stumble across a creek and decided to follow it upstream. He was completely unfamiliar with the area, so he made sure to mark his trail well. Eventually the creek took a wide turn, and just as he had hoped, the creek was a run off from the largest beaver colony that John had ever seen.

The runways of the colony's hauling trails were well laid to grade and purpose. The runs were wide and big enough to send a canoe down. The freshly cut trees, with their large teeth marks, were enough to tell him that he was sitting in a trapper's paradise. No wonder the Indians kept this place so secret; the beaver there were as big as dogs and twice as fat.

But the beaver colony wasn't the only thing that John found that day. All about the area were totems and symbols of an Indian burial ground. John clearly understood that being there could only bring trouble. But if it was trouble those Indians wanted, they need go no farther, because John was not about to leave the trapping grounds that he had spent a lifetime trying to find.

The next few weeks were spent laying out traps and collecting the finest bundle of furs this side of the Canadian border. But winter was not far off, and soon he would have to prepare for his trip downstream to the trading post. John was sure the other trappers would be as green as river moss when they laid their eyes on this set of furs. For the first time since John came to that region, he actually looked forward to going to the trading post.

But as it so often happens, John's jubilation was to be short-lived. One morning as John made his way up the creek to check his trapline, he found the trouble he knew would come. There in his path were two crossed war lances, the type common to the Indians of the area. He knew what the lances meant: The Indians were warning him not to go any farther. But they weren't going to scare John away from collecting the pelts that he worked so hard to get. So he went on to check the first of his traps. John didn't have to get very close before he knew there would be no beaver caught in this trap. Even from a distance he could see the Indian lance that stood erect where his trap should have been, a further warning for him to stay away. Big John felt no fear, but rather he was enraged at the thought that the local natives would dare defile his traps.

John hurried along his route, checking each of his traps, only to find that each had been opened or broken, each with a lance stuck through the center. By the time he made it to the burial grounds where the last of his traps were placed and finding these also destroyed, John was crazy with anger. And when that anger had fully consumed him, he screamed out at the forest horizon, vowing to avenge the wrongs done to him. But no sooner had the words left his mouth, than his eyes looked up at the ridge that kept guard over the valley from the north. There, mounted on their war ponies, sat three young braves, their faces painted in bright colors, shields and lances at their sides. All was quiet except the faint echoes of John's vow fading in the distance. The eyes of the four men locked on one another.

Suddenly the raging anger that had consumed John's mind spilled forth in a floodlike stream of curses and vows of eternal vengeance. John raised his rifle above his head, shook it at them, and challenged the three warriors to come and meet his wrath.

His challenge was answered in a heartbeat. The brave on the chestnut pony raised his lance, let out a war whoop, and came charging down into the valley directly at John. As he raised his rifle, John almost had to smile at how simple it was going to be, and with a single shot, the young warrior died halfway down the hill.

But no sooner had the shot rang out, than the brave atop a large gray pony let out a blood-curdling scream and came charging into the valley. John had started to reload but soon realized there was not enough time, so he dropped his rifle and quickly pulled his pistol from his belt. By the time John turned to shoot, the brave was nearly on top of him, leaving no time to get off a good shot. The bullet struck the Indian in the midsection, knocking him from his mount, at the same time his lance cut into John's side, twisting him to the ground. John's wound was not severe, and luckily the lance did not stick. The warrior was quick to get up and came at John with knife in hand. But the young brave's wound slowed him down. It was John's knife that found its mark first, and the young brave fell dead.

John struggled to his feet, and his eyes turned toward the last of the three braves. Their eyes met, and even at that distance, John could tell that this warrior was different from the others. Although young, John could see that the brave had fought in many battles by the tokens that hung from his war lance. He was more experienced than the other two.

The brave seemed to wait for John to regain his balance and prepare himself for the fight that was about to come. It was John who made the first move. He quickly reached for his rifle, hoping to be able to reload in time. The brave reacted quickly, and letting out a war whoop, he charged down the trail with his lance and shield at the ready. John worked feverishly to reload, but the charging warrior would not allow him enough time, for with a mighty heave, the Indian threw the lance and John made a quick move to his right, avoiding the lance by only inches. It stuck in the ground at the big man's feet. As John twisted around, he could see the warrior spin his pony about. The feathered warrior drew his tomahawk and prepared to make another charge. John reached out for the only weapon he had available, the Indian's own lance. He grabbed the lance firmly, set his feet, and waited for the brave to charge.

John's eyes were fixed and glowed with anger as the thundering pony closed down on him. John lashed out with the lance, only to have it glance off the young brave's shield. The warrior quickly turned his war pony and charged again. Again John lashed out with the lance, only this time it shattered as it struck the shield. The force threw John to the ground. John rolled, trying to get to his feet. He could hear the Indian's pony pulling up and turning for another pass. Seeing his rifle, John lunged for it, grabbed it on the roll, and somehow managed to get to his feet. Holding the rifle by the barrel, he waited for the next charge.

John's eyes were set with anger, his mind ablaze with hate! He cursed and challenged the brave to come at him again. The young warrior turned and pulled up his pony. Looking at the intruder, the Indian's eyes also filled with anger. Letting out a war whoop and kicking his pony, he charged again, his tomahawk at the ready. Just as the brave converged on him, John made a move to the right and swung the rifle with all his might, striking the Indian across the chest. The blow knocked the Indian from his mount and spun the big man to the ground.

John rolled, trying to get to his feet, his body not doing what his mind asked. He managed to get on his hands and knees and looked over to his foe. With a knife in hand, the young Indian warrior was also trying to regain his feet. He, too, was looking toward his foe. Slowly they rose to their feet and, standing face-to-face, knew this would be the final battle for one of them.

John was much larger than his foe, but the Indian was quicker. If John had fought anyone tougher in his life, he couldn't remember who it was. The battle seemed to go on forever. Both men were cut, bruised, bleeding, and near exhaustion. But the fight went on, neither giving ground to the other.

Finally the big man's strength won out, and John held the knife to the throat of the brave who had fought so hard. Without blinking so much as an eyelash, and with more strength than John knew he had left, he cut the Indian's throat so deeply that he severed the Indian's head from his body. John decided to keep the head as a totem.

After tending his wounds, John wrapped the head in a leather sack, gathered his gear, and slowly made his way back to his cabin. He was totally exhausted when he collapsed on his bed. His last thoughts as he drifted off were that he needed to get to the trading post and have his wounds tended to properly, that he would pack his furs and make the trip as soon as he awoke.

Sleep didn't bring the rest that John had hoped for. He tossed and turned all night, sometimes hot, other times cold. At some time in the gray of the morning, that void between the end of night and the beginning of day, John half awoke. There next to him stood an Indian. He appeared to be a medicine man, shaking a rattle and chanting something that John couldn't understand. Everything seemed like a dream. John's mind was too exhausted to interpret what was going on; he passed back into the darkness of sleep.

John awoke with a startle, the events of the night before still fuzzy in his brain. As he tried to clear his mind, John made his way to the cabin door. A breath of fresh air might help clear his head. His body ached and his wounds hurt as he crossed the floor. The sunlight nearly blinded him as he opened the door.

But John wasn't ready for what awaited him outside. There on the porch of his cabin were the shattered lance and the shield of the slain warrior. Not ten paces away lay the headless body wrapped in a blanket and covered with beads and trinkets.

The shock of what he saw shook John's already confused mind. Almost as if in a trance, he slowly walked toward the body. He couldn't understand why the Indians would bring the remains here. They could have buried him where he fell in their burial grounds. As John drew closer, he became aware of a smell, noxious, like an unclean hide hung to dry in the sun.

Suddenly, almost as if a sixth sense warned him, John spun around. There, only a few steps from him, stood the medicine man he had seen the previous night. Slowly, softly so John wouldn't miss a word, he spoke. John could understand most of what he said because he had had dealings with the Miami tribe, which lived in these parts. And although the language seemed the same, it was a different dialect.

It seemed that the young brave was the son of a tribal chief from the north, perhaps a cousin to the great warrior chief, Tecumseh. And befitting his position, he deserved a burial with many great gifts and tokens. But he needed to be buried whole, for without his head he would not be able to find his way to the next world. If John did not return his head willingly, the great warrior would wander forever between the two worlds. And many bad things would befall John the remainder of his days. With that the Indian was gone, leaving John standing trancelike in front of his cabin.

When he finally got a grip on himself, John turned to find that the body was also gone. Quickly he got back to the cabin, figuring that surely warriors would attack and take the head from him. And if they ever thought he would return that head of his own free will, they were sadly mistaken. Being as stubborn as he was, he figured that he'd give them a fight they'd never forget. John closed and barred all the windows and doors, gathered what little furnishing he had, and barricaded himself in.

Most of the day was spent with rifle in hand, with the head, still wrapped in the leather sack, next to him. Except for a few sudden outbursts of cussin' and swearin', John just sat there waiting for the Indians to return. Along about evening he built a fire, fixed himself something to eat, and again settled back and waited. He must have dozed off because all of a sudden he realized that the smell from the morning was back. Quickly he reached down and grabbed the sack next to him and threw it across the cabin. As it hit the floor, John heard the most gruesome moan he'd ever heard. It sent chills up his spine, and he moved away from the noise.

The moan came back, and as John looked in that direction, he saw the ghostly figure of an Indian standing in the corner. Dressed in buckskin and beads, he held in one arm his war lance and shield. In the other he held a headdress common to those parts. But above that Indian's shoulders there was nothing. There before John stood the headless apparition of the warrior he had slain.

John's heart felt as if it would jump clean out of his chest. The moaning seemed to get louder as the ghost seemed to float slowly toward John. He brought up his rifle and fired at the apparition, but the bullet went on through and struck the wall behind. John dropped the rifle and watched as the ghostly brave slowly raised his arms and cupped his hands in what appeared to be a pleading motion. John knew what the headless figure wanted. He had to force his body to move as he slowly crawled across the floor toward the sack he had thrown. Without taking his eyes off the spirit, he felt around until he found the sack and pulled it to his chest. As he

did, the moaning seemed to quiet a bit. John sat clutching the sack to his body, staring at the haunting figure
before him.

Suddenly, as if he had gone completely mad, John
started laughing, a wild hysterical laugh. He cursed and
swore at the brave and told him that he would not return
the head the ghost sought. And John dared the specter
to do his worst, for as long as he had the head there was
nothing that it could do to him.

Suddenly a banshee-like scream filled the room, the
fire flared up and as chilling a wind as John had ever felt
swirled about the cabin. Things flew about the room as
if they had minds of their own. The scream and moans
grew so load that it hurt the big man's ears. John curled
up on the floor, tucking the sack under him. Then, just as
suddenly, the place was quiet. John remained on the floor,
never looking up until the first rays of sunlight found
their way into the cabin.

Wasting no time, John packed his canoe and started
down the river. He figured if he really pushed and stayed
at it all day, he could make the trading post by late evening. With the leather sack tightly strapped to his side,
John paddled all day, never letting up. A strong current
got him to the post about an hour after dark.

He quickly made his way to the post. After downing
several large swallows of whiskey, John asked where he
could find Austin Handley, his one and only friend there.

John found his friend at a cabin on the north end of
the post. Over the better part of a bottle of whiskey, John
told Austin the entire story of the Indian head, even showing him the head he carried in the sack.

Now there's little doubt that Austin thought him completely mad, but he gave John a blanket and told him he could rest in the storage room that adjoined the cabin. Exhaustion and the drink made it easy for the big man to sleep.

Nobody knows for sure exactly why he awoke; it may have been the noxious smell or the sudden coldness that jolted John out of his sleep that night. But awake he was, and there standing over him was the ghost that now haunted him. Gone were the lance and shield. Nor did the apparition carry the headdress he had the previous night. But there was something else that the specter held. John tried to focus his eyes as the ghostly brave raised it to view. A large round item dangled from the hand of the ghostly arm. John looked harder at the object, and finally as his eyes adjusted, he could see that it looked familiar. Then a wave of sudden shock swept over him, his stomach twisted into a knot, his mouth opened for a scream that wouldn't come. John knew what the object was—it was the dismembered head of Austin Handley. John rolled and stumbled as he tried to get to his feet, his head spinning and his legs like rubber.

The big man finally made it to his feet. Wobbly and clutching the walls for support, he tried to find the door, the leather sack still hanging from his shoulder. As John stepped through the door, the Indian specter was already there waiting, laughing and holding the ghostly head of his only friend. John moved to the bed, still clutching the walls for support. There lying on the bed was the headless body of his friend.

The Indian Head

If Big John Walker had managed to keep his mind up to then, now he lost it. He ran screaming into the night, tearing through the brush, breaking his way through the branches like the madman most thought he was. He ran till his once powerful body would no longer do what his mind asked, and then he collapsed. There he lay, crying and still clutching the leather sack that carried his torment. Somehow he became aware of the faint sound of an Indian's rattle, the sound growing slowly closer, and John knew who was there. With a sudden calmness and sense of relief, he offered up the sack without even looking up. He felt it taken from his hand and heard the chanting of the medicine man. There he lay, first crying, then whimpering until unconsciousness took over his exhausted body.

When he awoke he was aware of a feeling of coldness—and the stench that had become all too familiar to him. He clutched at the now empty sack that had carried the Indian brave's head. As John opened his eyes, he saw the forest slowly revolving before him. And there on the ground was a body—a headless body. And John realized with a jolt that . . . IT WAS HIS OWN HEADLESS BODY. As John slowly turned his head, he found himself staring directly into the grinning face of the dead warrior. With a banshee yell the warrior flung John's head high into the air. With that, darkness came to Big John. It was the last sight he ever saw.

Story Outline

I. Big John Walker is a trapper in the early 1820s in Indiana, living not far from Fort Vincennes.

II. John Walker is half crazy, but he is the best trapper in the area. He finds a secret Indian trapping ground, but it is also part of a sacred burial ground.

III. He ignores the Indians' warnings not to trap there and is angered when they destroy his traps.

IV. Three braves accept his challenge to fight. Big John defeats the first two, shooting the first and wounding the second with his pistol and killing him after a fight. But he too is wounded.

V. Big John and the third Indian have a long and hard fight. At the end John gets the upper hand and cuts the Indian's throat so deeply that he severs the head from the body. John decides to keep the head as a victory totem.

VI. John treats his wounds, gathers his gear and furs, and returns to the cabin, planning to leave for the trading post for proper care as soon as he can.

VII. That night he tosses and turns in bed, and is finally awakened by a medicine man shaking a rattle and chanting. When morning comes, he still feels fuzzy and goes to the door for some fresh air.

VIII. There on the porch of the cabin are the shattered lance and shield of the slain warrior, and not ten paces away his headless body is wrapped in a blanket and covered with trinkets.

IX. A stench hangs in the air. John turns around and the medicine man is there, saying that the warrior needs to be given a funeral and that the head must be returned, or the brave will wander between this world and the next—and that a curse will be on John the rest of his days.

X. When John recovers from his shock, he sees that the medicine man and the body are gone.

XI. John stays ready with his gun all day, expecting the Indians to attack, but an attack never comes. After he eats supper that night, the headless warrior appears—amid a stench and feeling of cold—pleading for his head.

XII. John refuses the warrior's plea for his head— a banshee scream fills the air, the fire blazes, and then all is quiet.

XIII. Early the next day, Big John packs up and heads for Fort Vincennes, taking the head with him.

XIV. When he reaches the trading post, John looks up his one and only friend, Austin

Handley, and tells him the entire story. Handley allows him to sleep in a spare room that night.

XV. A cold feeling and the stench return that night, awakening Big John. When he opens his eyes, he sees that the headless brave's outstretched arm is holding the head of his friend Austin Handley.

XVI. Big John stumbles into the next room, and there on the bed lies the headless body of his friend.

XVII. John stumbles screaming from the cabin, carrying the leather sack with the Indian's head. The medicine man finds him, and this time John gives up the sack with a sense of relief.

XVIII. He collapses in the woods, exhausted. When John wakes up, he sees the forest revolving around him. Then he recognizes a headless body on the ground in front of him—IT IS HIS OWN HEADLESS BODY!

XIX. John slowly turns his head until he is facing the grinning face of the dead warrior. The warrior yells a war cry and throws John's head high into the air.

XX. Darkness then comes to Big John—it is the last sight that he will ever see.

9

THE NIGHTMARE TRAIL

by Scott E. Power

I considered myself a rational and sensible person until that night. I don't blame anyone for disbelieving me. I often don't believe it myself, but as soon as I close my eyes to sleep, there it is as vivid as that night. And as horrible.

I'm surprised at myself for trying to explain it all here again. I've told the story so many times. Each time people laugh in disbelief. I, too, would laugh if I heard such a story, if it had not happened to me. But it did. I can't deny it. If I hadn't been alone, maybe it wouldn't have happened at all. But I was, it did, and as a result, I will forever shun solitude.

Although I was anxious to arrive back at my cabin, which was only a mile down the river, I couldn't help but stop periodically to look around. All I could see through the falling snow was the riverbank and jagged tree line, the black spruces stabbing the dark sky with their twisted treetops. The whole panorama was illuminated by the soft light of the full moon, which was shining behind the thick cover of snow clouds. There was no sound. Only winter's silence literally humming in my ears. I have never understood how, when it is so silent in the north country, there seems to be a distant noise, not unlike the whine of a saw mill.

After a few moments of gazing at what appeared to be an enchanted fantasyland of a child's nightmare, which was really the frozen muskeg of northern Manitoba, I pressed on. The winter's silence was drowned out by the *CRUNCH . . . CRUNCH . . . CRUNCH* of the snow beneath my snowshoes.

I was contemplating the epicurean delight of a hot cup of tea back at my cabin when I saw the tracks. They were large tracks, but not the tracks that moose leave behind as they move through the snow. They resembled tracks made by a human. But who?

No one lived within fifty miles of my cabin. I didn't remember making the trail. It ran perpendicular to my trapline and to my normal travels. I could not think of a reason why I would have gone that way, unless to satisfy an urge to explore. But the trail was fresh, made within the last few hours. I hadn't seen it earlier while hiking past. Someone, or something, had just traveled through here. If so, it must have seen my trail. What was it? A human? If so, who was it? What were his intentions? Why was he traveling on such a stormy night?

As I pondered these questions, I felt the rhythm of my heartbeat rise to a staccato pounding. The only way to know the answer to this mystery was to follow the trail and find out. If worse came to worse, I had my rifle. But surely this was the trail of a fellow trapper whom I did not know. I turned off my trail and onto the other, following it into the dark gloom of the trees.

I had followed the trail into the woods a hundred yards or so when I began to see dark splotches on the snow. It was a substance I didn't recognize. The splotches were sporadic and of diverse sizes. I took off my gloves to touch them, attempting to identify them by their textures. But of course, the cold temperatures had already frozen the substance into grains of ice.

The thought crossed my mind that possibly blood had dripped from dead game that this unknown person had hunted. I felt comfortable with this thought and ceased to puzzle over it any longer.

I stopped to look over the surroundings. I could no longer see the river behind me. All about me were sinister shadows of gnarled black spruce. Occasionally, I would brush up against a tamarack tree. The cloud cover had begun to thin out, and the snow was changing into light flurries. The moonlight was swelling as the clouds dispersed.

The moon itself was full and ominous. The air seemed to be growing colder. I began to feel the frigid air stabbing me like pricking needles through my layers of wool and down. In the distance I heard the hunger cry of an Arctic wolf.

The trail I followed was longer than I had anticipated, and I began to feel as if it went nowhere specific. Just someone, or something, passing through. But that just seemed too outrageous; it had to be somewhere. Much to my surprise, as I continued trekking, I began to recognize various landmarks. I guess you could say I was experiencing a sense of déjà vu. I began to feel that I had been there before but didn't consciously remember it. It was like a dream, or a nightmare.

Finally, just over the sounds of the snow crunching beneath my snowshoes, I heard what seemed to be the song of a Canadian jay. But as I stopped to listen and discern, I realized it was the whistle of a human. At last I was nearing the mysterious person.

As I closed the distance between the whistler and myself, I began recognizing more and more of the surroundings. It was more eerie than bizarre. The hair on my neck stood up, and the gloom of the forest was serenaded by someone whistling in the darkness. It seemed to me that I was walking myself into a realm of paradox and surrealism. The atmosphere reeked with the warmth of evil and frigidity of death. I tried to convince myself to turn around and go home. But not knowing what was ahead, whistling in such a dreadful context, would forever vex me. Besides, I had come this far, and I did have my rifle.

The stains in the snow had become more frequent. I lit a match to examine them more closely. As the match flame illuminated the snow, I saw a dark crimson color. It was definitely blood.

Exactly at that moment, the tune being whistled in the distance changed. At first it had been merry and delightful, although I did not recognize the melody. But now the air was filled with the robust melancholy of Bach's "Toccata and Fugue." The sounds was amplified throughout the forest and resembled a pipe organ more than a whistle. But that was impossible, and I knew it. It was all in my head, made worse by my fatigue and terrible imagination.

I looked up from the ground and saw candlelight shining through a cabin window. A cabin! I couldn't believe it. I didn't think there was a cabin within fifty miles of my own. As I approached the cabin stealthily and with great curiosity, I began noticing that the cabin resembled mine. But it was difficult to concentrate and be sure, because the whistle was getting louder. It seemed to weaken me.

I was positive that the cabin looked like my own. The roof was an A-frame, the main cabin was about the same size, and there were windows on the east and west walls. And even more peculiar was the fact that the outhouse and woodshed were designed identically to mine.

Suddenly the person inside stopped whistling. My ears were ringing in its absence. My heart was pounding like a sledgehammer. Although the temperature was below zero, I was sweating. The trail of what I knew to be blood went around the corner of the cabin to the far side, where I assumed the entrance was. Just like mine.

I gazed through the window from where I sat, some twenty yards away, hoping to see who was inside this cabin. Unfortunately, I saw nobody, just a shadow dancing about in graceful glides. I unlashed my snowshoes, took hold of my gun, and prepared my nerve to go look through the window at the person inside.

As I sat there, I looked down at my hands, which grasped the rifle with a white-knuckled grip, and realized how ridiculous I was behaving. If someone was to have seen

The Nightmare Trail

me, he would have thought I was a child. I was ashamed. It was mere coincidence that this cabin resembled mine. It couldn't be mine. Besides, what did I think was in there? The windigo? The windigo is part of a Cree Indian legend that embodies all the fear, all the horror, and the wildness, starvation, misery, and terrible cold of the North. The windigo is supposedly a man and cannibal. But it is an Indian legend, not reality. It simply doesn't exist!

I laughed at myself and my imagination. It crossed my mind that I had lived in that God-forsaken land for too long and I was becoming "bushed," as they say in the North. I decided to leave my gun behind and simply go look inside the window to check things out. Then I would knock on the door and introduce myself. Maybe the person would be kind enough to offer me a cup of java. I certainly needed a warm drink. With a huge boost of confidence, I got up from where I sat and walked, as quietly as possible, to the window.

However, as I got closer, my determination began to melt away. I began noticing debris and other objects that I recognized. The spool of rope against the wall. The kerosene barrel. And just a few feet away, I could see a sled that looked like mine. This was my cabin! But how? Who was inside? And why the blood?

Immediately I grew weak with fright. Everything was too freakish for it to be normal. I felt I had fallen into a trap, and there was no way out. I remembered my rifle, but it was too late, I was at the window. I could delay no longer. I had to look in.

I peered in. Everything was as I had left it, but there was a fire burning in the stove, obviously started by this foreigner. And some kind of meat was being fried on the stove. Maybe that was what the blood came from.

I could see the person inside, but not the face. It was a man. He was tall and husky with long white hair. There was something hanging in the corner, but I couldn't tell what it was. The man moved the kerosene lantern onto a table by the stove, and I could make out a few more details. It was definitely meat of some sort cooking on the stove. But exactly what kind I couldn't tell. The carcass was still dripping blood, and under it was a bucket to catch the fluids. The carcass was hanging from its hind quarters, and the forelegs, minus the severed one, were almost touching the floor. It was a large animal, probably seven feet from tip to tip. The head had been severed.

The man, whose face I still could not see, removed the meat from the stove and, with his back to me, began to eat it. My eyes went back to the carcass. I tried to identify it. I was truly puzzled. Finally, as I let my eyes sweep over the room that was mine, I noticed something next to the lantern. The shadows on it cast from the light were sharp and full of contrast. It was difficult to discern what it was.

I stared and stared until the realization of its identity burned my consciousness with an evil that could only be from hell. My whole body quivered. My heart was overcome with fear. That thing in the shadows of my cabin was a human head! And the carcass was a human body!

I thought I was mad . . . insane . . . hallucinating. But there it was. Swinging in the shadows of my cabin. A bloody fresh carcass of a slaughtered human being.

The fear and horror of the evil overcame me. I wanted to run away, but I couldn't move. My whole body was paralyzed and sick.

The cannibalistic man inside stood up from the table where he was eating human flesh and walked toward the door. He was going outside! I must run! I turned to escape. As I did, I looked up and there he was in front of me! The windigo!

"You're next!" he shouted.

Darkness overcame me. I lost consciousness.

When I awoke, I was inside my cabin, tucked inside my warm sleeping bag. It was daylight. All was serene.

I looked around. No one was there. He, or it, was gone. Or had he even been there? There was no carcass, no head.

It was all a dream, a nightmare! My terrible ordeal was only a dream.

How good it was to be alive! Really alive! No fear, no horror. All was well.

After breakfast I had to check my trapline. As I left the cabin, I walked with a bounce, a joy of peace. But as I turned the river bend and approached the spot where my nightmare had started, I slowed with uncertainty. Had it truly been a dream, or not?

Yes! Of course it was a dream. I was still alive wasn't I?

But as I continued trekking, the scar of a freshly made trail perpendicular to mine became visible.

Story Outline

I. The narrator finds a mysterious trail leading into the woods, only about a mile from his cabin located in isolated wilderness.

II. As he follows it he notices splotches on the trail that he eventually finds to be blood.

III. He comes upon an inhabited cabin that he did not know existed.

IV. Initially scared, his fear increases when he notes that the cabin and its belongings appear to be identical to his own. He also notices a carcass hanging in the corner of the cabin.

V. To his horror, he realizes the body hung in the cabin, and being eaten by its inhabitant, is that of a human being.

VI. He then knows that he has come upon the windigo, the embodiment of all the fear, all the horror, all the wildness, starvation, misery, and terrible cold of the North.

VII. He turns to run from the cabin, but the windigo is suddenly right in front of him and shouts [and be sure to shout this when telling the story], "You're next!"

VIII. The narrator wakes up, safe in his cabin. It has only been a dream.

IX. After breakfast he leaves to check his trapline, and the story finishes with his noting a freshly made trail, perpendicular to his, just as in the dream.

10

THE BLOODY HAND

Anonymous, adapted by Doc Forgey

This anonymous legend was gleaned from a book of ghost stories. Generally these short stories do not lend themselves well to campfire telling, but I found this to be an exception.

In a certain village on the south coast, a widow and her two daughters were living in a house that stood rather apart from its neighbors on either side. It was situated on a wooded cliff, and about a quarter of a mile from its garden was a waterfall of some height. The two daughters were much attached to each other. One of them, Mary, was very attractive. Among her admirers were two men especially distinguished for their devotion to her. One of them, John Bodneys, seemed on the point of realizing the ambition of his life when a new competitor of a very different disposition appeared and completely conquered Mary's heart.

The day was fixed for the marriage, but though Mary wrote to the Bodneys family to announce her engagement and ask John to be present at her wedding, she had received no reply from him. On the evening before the wedding day, Ellen, the other sister, was gathering ferns in the woods when she heard a faint rustling behind her and, turning quickly around, thought she had a momentary glimpse of the figure of John Bodneys. Whoever it was vanished swiftly in the twilight. On her return to the house, Ellen told her sister what she thought she had seen, but neither of them thought much of it.

The wedding took place the next day. Just before the bride was due to leave with her husband, she took her sister to the room they had shared. It had a window that opened onto a balcony from which a flight of steps led down to the enclosed garden. After a few words, Mary said to her sister, "I would like to be alone for a few minutes. I will join you again presently."

Ellen left her and went downstairs, where she waited with the others. When half an hour had passed and Mary had not appeared, her sister went up to see if anything had happened to her. The bedroom door was locked. Ellen called but had no answer. Becoming alarmed, she ran downstairs and told her mother.

At last the door was forced open, but there was no trace of Mary in the room. They went into the garden, but except for a white rose lying on the path, they saw no sign of Mary. For the rest of that day and on the following days, they hunted high and low for Mary. The police were called in, the whole countryside was roused, but all to no purpose. Mary had utterly disappeared.

The years passed by. The mother and Mary's husband were dead, and of the wedding party only Ellen and an old servant were still alive. One winter's night the wind rose to a furious gale and did a great deal of damage to the trees near the waterfall. When workers came in the morning to clear away the fallen timber and fragments of rock, they found a skeleton hand, on the third finger of which was a wedding ring, guarded by another ring with a red stone in it. On searching further they found a complete skeleton, around whose bones some rags of clothes still adhered. The ring with the red stone in it was identified by Ellen as the one that her sister was wearing on her wedding day.

The skeleton was buried in the churchyard, but the shock of the discovery was so great that a few weeks later Ellen herself was on her deathbed. On the occasion of Mary's burial, she had insisted on keeping the skeleton hand with the rings, putting it in a glass box to secure it from accident. Now as she lay dying, she left the relic to the care of her old servant.

Shortly afterward the servant set up a hotel, where, as may be imagined, the skeleton hand and its story were a common topic of conversation among those who frequented its bar. One night a stranger, muffled up in a cloak, with a cap pulled over his face, made his way into the inn and asked for something to drink.

"It was a night like this when the great oak was blown down," the bartender observed to one of his customers.

"Yes," the other replied. "And it must have made the skeleton seem doubly ghastly, discovering it, as it were, in the midst of ruins."

"What skeleton?" asked the stranger, turning suddenly from the corner in which he had been standing.

"Oh, it's a long story," answered the publican. "You can see the hand in that glass case, and if you like, I will tell you how it came to be there."

He waited for the stranger's answer, but none came. The stranger was leaning against the wall in a state of collapse. He was staring at the hand, repeating again and again, "Blood, blood," and sure enough, blood was slowly dripping from his fingertips. A few minutes later, he had recovered sufficiently to admit that he was John Bodneys and to ask that he might be taken to the magistrate. He confessed to them that in a frenzy of jealousy, he had made his way into the private garden on Mary's wedding day. Seeing her alone in her room, he had entered and seized her, muffling her cries, and had taken her as far as the waterfall. There she had struggled so violently to escape from him that, unintentionally, he had pushed her off the rocks, and she had fallen into a cleft, where she was almost completely hidden. Afraid of being discovered, he had not even waited to find out whether she was dead or alive. He had fled and lived abroad ever since, until an overpowering longing led him to revisit the scene of his crime.

The Bloody Hand

After making his confession, Bodneys was committed to the county jail, where shortly afterward he died, before any trial could take place.

Story Outline

I. John Bodneys is very attracted to Mary, but she falls in love with someone else. She invites John to her wedding, but he does not reply.

II. Just before the bride is to leave with her husband, she goes upstairs to her room. But she never comes down! A search fails to find her.

III. Years pass, and everyone who had been at the wedding has died but her sister and an old servant. A storm destroys a large tree, whose roots pull up the remains of a woman in wedding clothes, with a wedding ring on her skeleton hand. The body is identified as Mary's.

IV. The body is buried in the churchyard, but her sister keeps the hand with its rings in a glass case. She soon dies and leaves the hand to the old servant.

V. The servant opens a tavern and hotel and displays the hand in a glass case.

VI. One day a stranger who overhears a conversation about the skeleton hand asks about it—the stranger stares at the hand and collapses.

VII. He admits to being John Bodneys and having killed Mary, leaving her in the crevasse by the old tree.

When telling this story, I do not have the hand dripping blood, as in the original version, but rather have John Bodneys recognize the rings and the hand as belonging to the murder victim and collapsing because of this grisly reminder from his past.

11

ONE SUMMER NIGHT

by Ambrose Bierce

This macabre tale by Ambrose Bierce is about a topic that all medical students have to encounter—the dead body required for dissection in anatomy class. In medieval Europe a copy of the keys to the city cemetery was a legacy passed from one medical school class to the next. Voluntary donations have now replaced body snatching, but this tale returns to the time—not so long ago—when medical students had to fend for themselves in this grisly business.

The fact that Henry Armstrong was buried did not seem to him to prove that he was dead: He had always been a hard man to convince. That he really was buried, the testimony of his senses compelled him to admit. His posture—flat upon his back, with his hands crossed upon his stomach and tied with something that he easily broke without profitably altering the situation—the strict confinement of his entire person, the black darkness and profound silence, made a body of evidence impossible to controvert, and he accepted it without cavil.

But dead—no; he was only very, very ill. He had, withal, the invalid's apathy and did not greatly concern himself about the uncommon fate that had been allotted to him. No philosopher was he—just a plain, commonplace person gifted, for the time being, with a pathological indifference: The organ that he feared consequences with was torpid. So, with no particular apprehension for his immediate future, he fell asleep and all was at peace with Henry Armstrong.

But something was going on overhead. It was a dark summer night, shot through with infrequent shimmers of lightning silently firing a cloud lying low in the west and portending a storm. These brief, stammering illuminations brought out with ghastly distinctness the monuments and headstones of the cemetery and seemed to set them dancing. It was not a night in which any credible witness was likely to be straying about a cemetery, so the three men who were there, digging into the grave of Henry Armstrong, felt reasonably secure.

Two of them were young students from a medical college a few miles away; the third was a gigantic Negro

One Summer Night

known as Jess. For many years Jess had been employed about the cemetery as a man-of-all-work, and it was his favorite pleasantry that he knew "every soul in the place." From the nature of what he was now doing, it was inferable that the place was not so populous as its register may have shown it to be.

Outside the wall, at the part of the grounds farthest from the public road, were a horse and a light wagon, waiting.

The work of excavation was not difficult: The earth with which the grave had been loosely filled a few hours before offered little resistance and was soon thrown out. Removal of the casket from its box was less easy, but it was taken out, for it was a perquisite of Jess, who carefully unscrewed the cover and laid it aside, exposing the body in black trousers and white shirt. At that instant the air sprang to flame, a cracking shock of thunder shook the stunned world and Henry Armstrong tranquilly sat up. With inarticulate cries the men fled in terror, each in a different direction. For nothing on earth could two of them have been persuaded to return. But Jess was of another breed.

In the gray of the morning the two students, pallid and haggard from anxiety and with the terror of their adventure still beating tumultuously in their blood, met at the medical college.

"You saw it?" cried one.

"God! Yes—what are we to do?"

They went around to the rear of the building, where they saw a horse, attached to a light wagon, hitched to a gate post near the door of the dissecting room. Mechanically they entered the room. On a bench in the obscurity sat Jess. He rose, grinning, all eyes and teeth.

"I'm waiting for my pay," he said.

Stretched naked on a long table lay the body of Henry Armstrong, the head defiled with blood and clay from a blow with a spade.

Story Outline

I. Henry Armstrong had been very ill and was buried alive—he can tell that when he wakes up.

II. Up above him it is a dark night, complete with flashes of summer lightning. Three men are in the cemetery, digging up the grave of Henry Armstrong. Two are medical students, the other is a big fellow named Jess who is employed at the cemetery—a person who steals bodies often.

III. It is easy digging into the newly dug grave. Lifting the coffin out is less easy.

IV. When the lid is removed, a crack of thunder shakes the air—and Henry Armstrong sits up in the coffin.

V. The three men run in terror in different directions. The medical students meet at the college early in the morning, still scared and haggard from their horrible night.

VI. They go to the dissecting room, and there is Jess who says, "I'm waiting for my pay."

VII. And on the table is the body of Henry Armstrong, his head crushed from a blow with a spade.

THE STRANGER

by Ambrose Bierce

*Some of Ambrose Bierce's tales of the super-
natural make particularly good campfire
stories—especially this one with its outdoors
setting, around a campfire in remote wilderness, about someone—or something—that
enters this group's lives.*

A man stepped out of the darkness into the little illuminated circle about our failing campfire and seated himself
upon a rock.

"You are not the first to explore this region," he said
gravely.

Nobody controverted his statement; he was himself
proof of its truth, for he was not of our party and must have
been somewhere near when we camped. Moreover, he must

have companions not far away; it was not a place where one would be living or traveling alone. For more than a week we had seen, besides ourselves and our animals, only such living things as rattlesnakes and horned toads. In an Arizona desert one does not long coexist with only such creatures as these; one must have pack animals, supplies, arms—"an outfit." And all these imply comrades. It was, perhaps, a doubt as to what manner of men this unceremonious stranger's comrades might be, together with something in his words interpretable as a challenge, that caused every man of our half a dozen "gentlemen adventurers" to rise to a sitting posture and lay his hand upon a weapon—an act signifying, in that time and place, a policy of expectation. The stranger gave the matter no attention and began again to speak in the same deliberate, uninflected monotone in which he had delivered his first sentence: "Thirty years ago Ramon Gallegos, William Shaw, George W. Kent, and Berry Davis, all of Tucson, crossed the Santa Catalina Mountains and traveled due west, as nearly as the configuration of the country permitted. We were prospecting, and it was our intention, if we found nothing, to push through to the Gila River at some point near Big Bend, where we understood there was a settlement. We had a good outfit but no guide, just Ramon Gallegos, William Shaw, George W. Kent, and Berry Davis."

The man repeated the names slowly and distinctly, as if to fix them in the memories of his audience, every member of whom was now attentively observing him, but with a slackened apprehension regarding his possible companions somewhere in the darkness that seemed to enclose us like a black wall, for in the manner of this volunteer historian was no suggestion of an unfriendly purpose. His act was rather that of a harmless lunatic than an enemy. We were not so new to the country as not to know that the solitary life of many a plainsman had a tendency to develop eccentricities of conduct and character not always easily distinguishable from mental aberration. A man is like a tree: In a forest of his fellows he will grow as straight as his genetic and individual nature permits; alone, in the open, he yields to the deforming stresses and tortions that environ him.

Some such thoughts were in my mind as I watched the man from the shadow of my hat, pulled low to shut out the firelight. A witless fellow, no doubt, but what could he be doing there in the heart of a desert?

Nobody having broken the silence, the visitor went on to say: "This country was not then what it is now. There was not a ranch between the Gila and the Gulf. There was a little game here and there in the mountains, and near the infrequent water holes grass enough to keep our animals from starvation. If we should be so fortunate as to encounter no Indians, we might get through. But within a week the purpose of the expedition had altered from discovery of wealth to preservation of life. We had gone too far to go back, for what was ahead could be no worse than what was behind; so we pushed on, riding by night to avoid Indians and the intolerable heat, and concealing ourselves by day as best we could. Sometimes, having exhausted our supply of wild meat and emptied our casks, we were days without food and drink; then a water hole or a shallow pool in the bottom of an arroyo so restored our strength and sanity that we were able to shoot some of the wild animals that sought it also. Sometimes it was a bear, sometimes an antelope, a coyote, a cougar—that was as God pleased; all were food.

"One morning as we skirted a mountain range, seeking a practicable pass, we were attacked by a band of Apaches who had followed our trail up a gulch—it is not far from here. Knowing that they outnumbered us ten to one, they took none of their usual cowardly precautions, but dashed upon us at a gallop, firing and yelling. Fighting was out of the question. We urged our feeble animals up the gulch as far as there was footing for a hoof, then threw ourselves out of our saddles and took to the chaparral on one of the slopes, abandoning our entire outfit to the enemy. But we retained our rifles, every man—Ramon Gallegos, William Shaw, George W. Kent, and Berry Davis."

"Same old crowd," said the humorist of the party. A gesture of disapproval from our leader silenced him, and the stranger proceeded with his tale:

"The savages dismounted also, and some of them ran up the gulch beyond the point at which we had left it, cutting off further retreat in that direction and forcing us on up the side. Unfortunately the chaparral extended only a short distance up the slope, and as we came into the open ground above, we took the fire of a dozen rifles; but Apaches shoot badly when in a hurry, and God so willed it that none of us fell. Twenty yards up the slope, beyond the edge of the brush, were vertical cliffs, in which, directly in front of us, was a narrow opening. Into that we ran, finding ourselves in a cavern about as large as an ordinary room. Here for a time we were safe. A single man with a repeating rifle could defend the entrance against all the

Apaches in the land. But against hunger and thirst we had no defense. Courage we still had, but hope was a memory.

"Not one of those Indians did we afterwards see, but by the smoke and glare of their fires in the gulch we knew that by day and by night they watched with ready rifles in the edge of the bush—knew that, if we made a sortie, not a man of us would live to take three steps into the open. For three days, watching in turn, we held out, before our suffering became insupportable. Then—it was the morning of the fourth day—Ramon Gallegos said,

"'Señores, I know not well of the good God and what please him. I have lived without religion, and I am not acquainted with that of yours. Pardon, señores, if I shock you, but for me the time is come to beat the game of the Apache.'

"He knelt upon the rock floor of the cave and pressed his pistol against his temple. 'Madre de Dios,' he said, 'comes now the soul of Ramon Gallegos.'

"And so he left us—William Shaw, George W. Kent, and Berry Davis.

"I was the leader. It was for me to speak.

"'He was a brave man,' I said. 'He knew when to die, and how. It is foolish to go mad from thirst and fall by Apache bullets, or be skinned alive—it is in bad taste. Let us join Ramon Gallegos.'

"'That is right,' said William Shaw.

"'That is right,' said George W. Kent.

"I straightened the limbs of Ramon Gallegos and put a handkerchief over his face. Then William Shaw said: 'I should like to look like that a little while.'

"And George W. Kent said that he felt that way too.

"'It shall be so,' I said. 'The devils will wait a week. William Shaw and George W. Kent, draw and kneel.'

"They did so and I stood before them.

"'Almighty God, our Father,' said I.

"'Almighty God, our Father,' said William Shaw.

"'Almighty God, our Father,' said George W. Kent.

"'Forgive us our sins,' said I.

"'Forgive us our sins,' said they.

"'And receive our souls.'

"'And receive our souls.'

"'Amen!'

"'Amen!'

"I laid them beside Ramon Gallegos and covered their faces."

There was a quick commotion on the opposite side of the campfire. One of our party had sprung to his feet, pistol in hand.

"And you!" he shouted. "You dared to escape? You dare to be alive? You cowardly hound, I'll send you to join them if I hang for it!"

But with the leap of a panther the captain was upon him, grasping his wrist. "Hold it in, Sam Yountsey, hold it in!"

We were now all upon our feet, except for the stranger, who sat motionless and apparently inattentive. Someone seized Yountsey's other arm.

"Captain," I said, "there is something wrong here. This fellow is either a lunatic or merely a liar—just a plain, everyday liar that Yountsey has no call to kill. If this man was of that party it had five members, one of whom—probably himself—he has not named."

The Stranger

"Yes," said the captain, releasing the insurgent, who sat down, "there is something—unusual. Years ago four dead bodies of white men, scalped and shamefully mutilated, were found about the mouth of that cave. They are buried there; I have seen the graves—we shall all see them tomorrow."

The stranger rose, standing tall in the light of the expiring fire, which in our breathless attention to his story we had neglected to keep going.

"There were four," he said. "Ramon Gallegos, William Shaw, George W. Kent, and Berry Davis."

With this reiterated roll call of the dead, he walked into the darkness, and we saw him no more.

At that moment one of our party, who had been on guard, strode in among us, rifle in hand and somewhat excited.

"Captain," he said, "for the last half an hour three men have been standing out there on the mesa." He pointed in the direction taken by the stranger. "I could see them distinctly, for the moon is up, but as they had no guns and I had them covered with mine, I thought it was their move. They have made none, but damn it! They got on my nerves."

"Go back to your post, and stay till you see them again," said the captain. "The rest of you lie down again, or I'll kick you all into the fire."

The sentinel obediently withdrew, swearing, and did not return. As we were arranging our blankets, the fiery Yountsey said: "I beg your pardon, Captain, but who the devil do you take them to be?"

"Ramon Gallegos, William Shaw, and George W. Kent."

"But how about Berry Davis? I ought to have shot him."

"Quite needless; you couldn't have made him any deader. Go to sleep."

The original story glosses over the fact that Berry Davis sat with the dead bodies of his friends a full week before he killed himself, so that his friends could rest unmutilated by Indians "for a little while" as requested by William Shaw and George W. Kent. I generally make more a point of this when telling the story—actually drawing out his staying in the hot cave with his dead friends, holding off the Indians' attacks, and starving until he could stand it no longer—then killing himself.

Story Outline

I. A group of cowboys is seated around a campfire in Arizona when a stranger steps into the light of their fire and tells them a story.

II. He relates how Ramon Gallegos, William Shaw, George W. Kent, and Berry Davis had been prospecting in that area many years before.

III. They nearly starved and died from thirst as they struggled through the unexplored desert, shooting what game they could find at water holes.

IV. They traveled by night to avoid the heat and Indians, but their luck ran out one morning when a band of Apaches caught up with them and trapped them in a gully.

V. The men found refuge from Indian bullets in a cave but were trapped without food or water.

VI. After three days they could stand it no longer, and Ramon Gallegos said he did not want to be tortured by thirst and hunger and shot himself.

VII. His body was laid out with a handkerchief over his face. William Shaw and George W. Kent said that they would like to look like that without being mutilated by the Indians, if only for a little while. Their leader said, "It shall be so. The devils will wait a week."

VIII. The two men were laid out alongside Ramon Gallegos, their faces covered.

IX. Some of the cowboys think that this man escaped the massacre and abandoned his friends, or that he is a fifth member of this group.

X. The cowboy foreman says that four mutilated bodies were found at a cave entrance near where they are camping many years ago, and that their graves are close by.

XI. The stranger repeats that there were only four in the party—and again gives their names. He then leaves the camp.

XII. The guard comes in and says he noted three men just standing outside of their camp. He is told to return to his guard duty, and the rest of the men are ordered to bed.

XIII. The foreman is asked who the three men are, and he answers, "Ramon Gallegos, William Shaw, and George W. Kent." When a cowboy says he should have shot the cowardly Berry Davis, the foreman answers, "Quite needless; you couldn't have made him any deader. Go to sleep."

If you have trouble remembering the slain men's names, try substituting the names of relatives or coworkers.

13

THE MANOR

Sir Walter Scott, adapted by Pat Sherwood

This story is an adaptation of an old Sir Walter Scott story by the same name. It has been placed in a modern setting to provide more relevance for the campfire audience. Some old stories, such as "The Stranger," are best left in their ancient settings, while others seem to work better with modernization.

The road and the scenery whizzed by, but the country's beauty was lost to the driver. His thoughts weren't on the local charms or even on the destination for which the car was headed; his mind was on a war, a war in a faraway land.

But the war was over for Lt. Col. Brad Rallings; at least the combat was over. A Viet Cong land mine had seen to that. It was strange the way things had turned out. He was one of the few who had become exactly what he had always wanted to be, a combat officer. Now he would finish his career behind a desk at a training command, a career that had taken him through four tours of Viet Nam, earned him a chest full of medals and now a leg that would never function as it should again. Yeah, it was strange the way things turned out sometimes.

A sudden curve in the road brought him back to reality, and the colonel took notice of the picturesque countryside that was all around him. His thoughts turned to his destination and a friend he had not seen since he first entered the service. It would be great seeing his childhood buddy again. He and Ken had been chums since they were old enough to walk. They did everything together. They were even roommates in college. Ken went into business, and Brad entered the military. But they had always kept in contact with each other, no matter where their careers took them.

Ken had inherited an old country manor a few years back. Actually it was more of an estate. Ken had converted it into a resort, the opening of which occurred just a few weeks earlier. Now that the colonel had several weeks of medical leave, he couldn't think of a better place to recuperate than at a quiet manor out in the country. Three weeks of total peace and quiet would hopefully give him a new frame of mind with regard to his new command behind a desk.

The road wound through the countryside like a shiny ribbon, enshrouded on either side by thick green woods, which, from time to time, gave way at different points to offer the eye a fleeting glimpse of the truly magnificent scenery. It was through one of these woodland portholes that the colonel first caught sight of the manor. The colonel stopped his car and gazed across the valley at the manor resting sedately on the side of the adjacent hill. The sight was enough to bring a sense of calm to the haggard soldier's mind. His heart warmed at the thought of his lifelong friend in possession of such a delightful place. He couldn't picture a better place to rest up before returning to his duties as a soldier. He quickly pulled away, now anxious to see his friend and get settled in for a much needed rest.

On his arrival the colonel was greeted by a porter, who when learning his identity, quickly sent word of his arrival to the owner. As he waited, the colonel looked about in awe. The manor was even more splendid than he had imagined. It was then that the colonel first saw Ken, and although the years had been many, he instantly recognized him. But for a moment his childhood friend seemed to hesitate and looked at him like a stranger. Col. Rallings had the face of a soldier, upon which war with its fatigues and wounds had made a great alteration. But the uncertainty lasted only until the colonel spoke. The hearty greeting that followed was one that could only be shared between those who had spent countless days of childhood and early youth together.

"If I had but one wish," said the soldier's friend, "it would be that you had been here to share the opening of my manor!"

The colonel made a suitable reply and congratulated his friend on the fine manor he had acquired.

"You ain't seen nothing yet, ole buddy!" his friend replied and proceeded to give the colonel a personally guided tour of the manor.

"Don't think that your exploits haven't been watched," Ken told him at one point. "I've kept close track of your career, and a glorious one it's been. Twice decorated for valor, a Distinguished Service Cross, and so many more honors that I can't count them all."

The tour ended when they came to an isolated area of the manor. The colonel's friend led him down a hallway that ended in front of a large oak door that strangely did not match the rest of the decor. "This is part of the original manor," his friend explained, "It's much like it was when the house was first built, and I've reserved it especially for you. Now why don't you freshen up. I'll see you for dinner at about eight in the dining room." With that the owner of the manor took his leave.

The colonel found the room to be something right out of the 1800s, with heavy ornate wood trim and plastered walls. The furnishings were antique and centered around a very large four-poster bed. All in all the room was quite nice and seemed the perfect place to relax.

After unpacking, the colonel took a stroll on the large balcony that ran the length of the manor and adjoined his room. He had access to it by way of two large patio doors. He felt relaxed and comfortable. The colonel looked forward to dinner with his friend.

A celebration took place that evening in the dining hall. Ken had prepared a special banquet in the colonel's honor, and it was attended by many of the owner's friends and guests. The soldier was introduced as a man of great honor and bravery. His exploits and awards were revealed to those attending, and the colonel was coaxed by his host to speak of his adventures. All who were present looked on the soldier as a brave officer, one who was sensible, cool under fire, and who had gained the respect of his fellow officers and the men who fought under him.

After dinner the evening turned to entertainment and dancing. The atmosphere was that of a relaxed party. The festivities ended at a respectable hour, and the guests returned to their rooms. The host accompanied the colonel to his room, and when they reached the door, he inquired if his friend found his accommodations to his liking. The colonel answered that it was most comfortable, and because it was the property of such a dear friend, he would rather be here than anywhere else. The two childhood friends bid each other good night with a warm handshake. "I'll see you at breakfast promptly at eight," his host said as he retreated down the hall.

The colonel entered his room, looked around, and thought to himself how different it was here, how comfortable compared with the hardships and pain he had suffered the past few weeks. With this he prepared himself for bed and a luxurious night's sleep.

The next morning found the host and a few friends assembled for breakfast at eight without the colonel. Because he was the desired guest, his absence was justly noticed. More than once Ken expressed his surprise at the soldier's lack of promptness and finally sent a porter to check on the colonel. The porter came back to inform him that the colonel was not in his room and had been seen walking about the terrace and grounds since very early that morning, which seemed strange because the weather had turned cold and misty.

"Just like a soldier," said the host to those around the table. "Many of them have the habit of not sleeping past light because their duty calls for them to be alert at early hours." But his explanation didn't really sit well with Ken, and he soon excused himself to find his boyhood friend. Ken found the colonel as the porter had said, roaming aimlessly about the grounds. The colonel looked extremely fatigued and feverish. His clothes were wrinkled and hung on him with a careless negligence that was surprising for a military man. His hair was mussed and damp with dew, his face haggard and ghastly in some strange way.

"You look absolutely horrible this morning, Brad," commented Ken with some concern. "Are you feeling all right? Why were you wandering around so early this morning? You okay?"

"I'm fine," the colonel replied quickly, but with the air of embarrassment that made it obvious that he was not telling the truth.

"Why don't you come in and get a cup of coffee and eat some breakfast. You'll feel better," Ken said.

"No thanks, Ken," answered the colonel with a quiver in his voice. With a hesitation that didn't go unnoticed, the colonel said that he had asked the porter to collect his bags and bring his car around.

"Why?" asked Ken with surprise. "You said you'd spend at least a couple of weeks. Why the sudden change of heart?"

"I'm sorry, Ken. I know it's sudden, but I must get to my next command," announced the much-decorated soldier with obvious embarrassment. "That's a bunch of bull, and you know it!" his friend said firmly. "Now level with me, what happened last night that has you so rattled?"

After a long hesitation the colonel turned and looked into the eyes of the man with whom he had shared his childhood and who was undoubtedly his best friend. It was then that Ken noticed something he had never before seen in the eyes of this modern-day warrior. He saw fear!

"Brad, as my oldest and dearest friend and on the honor of a soldier, I want you to answer me honestly: How did you sleep last night?" asked the owner of the manor.

There was once again a long hesitation. Then with a sigh of resignation, the brave colonel answered, "I've never in my life spent such a horrible night. It was so miserable that I couldn't run the risk of spending another night, not for anything, not even for you."

"This is unbelievable," said the host as if speaking to himself. Ken turned back to the colonel and said, "For God's sake, Brad, be candid and tell me everything that happened last night. Tell me what could possibly have done this to you."

The colonel seemed very distressed by his friend's request and paused at length before he replied. "Ken, what happened last night was so bizarre and frightening that I wouldn't want to recount it to anybody, not even you. But I feel somehow honor bound to tell you what happened. If I told anyone else they would think I had completely flipped out, but you know me, and you should know that

I would never make up something as unthinkable as what I'm about to tell you."

With this the colonel paused and looked directly into the eyes of his friend.

"Believe me Brad, I know there's something really bothering you. I know that you'll be telling the truth no matter how strange it sounds!" replied Ken. "Now tell me what happened."

"All right," said the veteran soldier, "I'll tell you as best I can, relying on your discretion; and yet I'd rather face a company of Viet Cong than recall what happened last night!"

The brave colonel paused again; Ken's silence confirmed his attention and willingness to hear him out. So with great reluctance and a sense of uneasiness, the colonel related the events of the worst night in his life.

"After you left me last night, I got ready for bed. The fire in the hearth burned brightly, and I lay thinking of our childhood and growing up, how our lives had changed over the years. All of these were fond memories. I was glad to be here, spending this time with my best friend." Again the colonel paused, then almost forcing himself, he continued. "I was just about to doze off, when I was aroused by the sound of footsteps, like that a woman would make in high heels as she walked across the floor. I could also hear the rustling of material, like a woman's gown would make. As I sat up in bed and focused my eyes, I saw the figure of a woman pass in front of the fireplace. Her back was to me, but by the way she held herself, her neck, her shoulders, I could tell that it was an old woman whose dress was an old-fashioned gown, like those you see in a movie about the Civil War."

The colonel closed his eyes for a moment, then cleared his throat to continue. "I really didn't think much of the intrusion. I figured it to be no more than an elderly (perhaps senile) guest who was confused as to the room in which she belonged. So I shifted myself to accommodate my injured leg and coughed to let her know I was there. That's when she slowly turned toward me. I swear, Ken, nothing in my life prepared me for what I saw." The soldier's eye looked skyward, and Ken could see the fear that was in them as his friend forced himself to continue. "There wasn't any doubt as to what she was, or even any chance that she was still among the living. Her face had the fixed features of a corpse, yet somehow manifested the vile, hideous passions she possessed while alive. Her form was like some demonic soul that the Devil sent back from the grave! Some fiendish creature whose guilt was too great to lie quietly in eternity. In my horror I pushed myself backward to the head of the bed, supporting myself on my palms. Too scared to move, I watched as this hideous specter, in what seemed a single move, climbed right onto the bed. No more than a foot away from me, she squatted over the top of me. Her eyes were wide and wild, as if she was completely insane. Her grin was that of demonic maniac, mocking and full of malice."

Here the colonel stopped and wiped away the cold beads of sweat that had formed during the recalling of that horrible night. His breathing was labored, and he tried to calm himself before he went on.

"My Lord, Ken," the colonel continued in a trembling voice. "I'm no coward. I've proven that a hundred times on the battlefield, and I've never dishonored myself or my

The Manor

men. But having this thing hovering over me with those horrible demonic eyes and being so close that . . . that horrid evil incarnation . . ." He paused to recapture his labored breath. "I . . . I couldn't control my fear. My blood seemed to turn to ice. The hair stood up on the back of my neck, and I shook with panic . . . that's when I must have passed out."

The soldier's head seemed to fall in shame. When he again spoke, his voice was weak and shaky, "How long I was out I couldn't tell you."

The haggard soldier, the person that Ken was sure possessed no fear, slowly walked a few steps and gazed out over the terrace, gathering himself before going on with his terrible story.

"When I finally came to, I lay with my eyes closed for some time for fear of seeing that horrible hag hovering above me once again. When I finally gathered enough courage to look, she was no longer there. It's to my own shame that I'll tell you, I was so afraid of crossing paths with that terrible creature again that I lay huddled in that bed, too afraid to get out. I can't even begin to tell you of the hideous things that ran through my mind as I lay there waiting for dawn. But those were all in my mind; I knew the difference. At first light of day I quickly threw on my clothes and got out of that haunted room. I wandered the grounds trying to soothe my nerves. Now you know why I can't spend another night under the same roof with that demon hag."

As strange as the colonel's tale was, Ken had no doubt as to the conviction in his friend's recollection of the previous night. He never questioned the possibility that it all could have been a bad dream. Quite the contrary, Ken didn't seem to doubt a single word of the soldier's tale. A look of sorrow and regret had taken over his normally jovial face.

"I'm truly sorry for the pain and anguish you have suffered," Ken began slowly, "for I'm afraid I'm to blame for what happened last night! That room I gave you last night has been closed up for many, many years because it was said to be haunted. When I inherited the manor, I reopened the room, not believing at all that it was haunted. Everybody around here knows of the room, and I figured that they would be biased toward it and rekindle the rumors if they were to spend the night there. So when you called and said you were coming, I thought it the perfect opportunity to dispel the rumors and make the room useful again. Your courage is indisputable, and with no prior knowledge of the room, you were perfect for my little experiment."

"Thanks a lot, Ken" said the colonel, somewhat hastily. "I'll be forever in your debt, as I'm likely to remember for some time the consequences of your so-called little experiment. Next time, find some other guinea pig!"

"Now you're being unfair, Brad," Ken said. "I would never have put you through that if for a moment I believed it would cause you so much grief. You know that. If I had told you ahead of time, you would have jumped at the chance to stay in that room. Perhaps I was wrong in my method, but what happened last night was not my fault. You must remember that until this morning, I honestly didn't believe that the room was haunted."

"You're right, Ken," said the colonel, the anger no longer in his voice. "I know I have no right to be mad at you. Until last night I didn't believe in ghosts either and most likely would have taken that room if you had told me. Look, I see that my car's here, and I don't want to keep you from your guests any longer, so I'll be going now."

"Brad, wait. I know there's no way I can talk you into remaining now, but can't you stay for a while? There are some things that I want to show you," pleaded the colonel's friend.

The shaken colonel accepted the invitation, although somewhat reluctantly. Brad Rallings would not breathe easy until he was far away from this manor, but he owed it to his lifelong friend to at least grant his request.

The colonel followed his host through several rooms and into a long gallery hung with portraits, which Ken pointed out were his ancestors and former owners of the manor. As they moved down the gallery, Ken would point out certain paintings, telling their names and giving some account of who they were. The colonel had little interest but followed along quietly. They were about halfway down the gallery when Ken noticed that the colonel suddenly stiffened and jumped back in the utmost surprise and not without some fear, if the way his eyes were riveted to a portrait of an old lady in a sacque, the fashionable dress of the end of the seventeenth century, were any indication.

"There she is!" he exclaimed. "That's her, the woman from the room! Not as hideous as last night, but it's her nonetheless!"

"If that's the case," said the colonel's friend, "there's no doubt as to the horrible reality of your ghost. That is a picture of a wretched ancestress of mine. Her crimes are too numerous to count, too horrible to name. Let's just say that the crimes committed in that room were unnatural acts of violence and death. I will reseal the room, leaving it to the isolation to which the better judgment of those before me consigned it; and never again, as long as I can help it, will anyone go through the anguish that you have."

Thus the two friends who had met with such happiness, parted in very different moods: Ken to dismantle the haunted room and have it sealed; and the colonel to finish out his career, hoping to forget that horrifying night he passed while at the manor.

Story Outline

I. A wounded Vietnam war hero, Lt. Col. Brad Rallings, is home on sick leave and plans to visit a high school friend whom he has not seen for years.

II. His friend, Ken, inherited an old country manor and has turned it into a resort, inviting Brad to spend several weeks there to aid in his recuperation.

III. The colonel is the guest of honor at dinner. Everyone admires the war hero and gives him great respect because of his demonstrated heroism.

IV. Ken takes the colonel to the special guest room that has been prepared for him, a room strangely isolated in an unused portion of the old manor house.

V. The next morning the colonel fails to appear for breakfast. When Ken finds him wandering outside, the colonel appears fatigued and rumpled.

VI. Ken asks him how he slept and finally learns that the brave colonel has just spent the most terrifying night of his life.

VII. The colonel relates that just as he was falling asleep, he heard the footsteps of a woman.

VIII. He could see an old woman pass between him and the fireplace. Thinking that she was a guest who had wandered accidentally into his room, he coughed to let her know he was there.

IX. But an evil, dead creature turned toward him and leaped upon his bed, causing him to feel such concentrated horror that he became paralyzed with fear and passed out.

X. When he awoke, he was afraid to open his eyes, fearing that the hideous face would still be hovering over him.

XI. He stayed frozen in fright until dawn appeared, when he immediately threw on his clothes and left the mansion to soothe his nerves.

XII. His friend apologizes for placing him in the haunted room but points out that he needed someone with great courage, who had not heard of the ghost, to test the room and find the truth.

XIII. Ken then tells the colonel that he had to show him something. Taking him on a tour of the manor, he shows him a series of family portraits. Suddenly the colonel recognizes one as being that of the woman whose ghost he had seen the night before.

XIV. Ken tells the colonel that she had been an evil wretch, and that she had committed horrible crimes in that room. He swears that he will seal the room forever so that no one will ever again have to experience the fear that his friend did.

THE COMPANION

by Pat Sherwood

As a scoutmaster, a hunter, and an outdoorsman, I've become accustomed to being in the woods after dark, and I usually walk the trails around my campsite without the aid of a light. I believe most people who spend any amount of time in the outdoors grow to expect the unexpected from time to time and condition themselves to deal with such things. But even the most experienced outdoorsperson can't be ready for everything.

It was a moonless night in the latter part of August and the second night in camp for Troop 76. The fading embers of the campfire indicated the lateness of the night. All the Scouts were safely tucked into their sleeping bags, and the leaders were just settling into theirs. The only one that remained outside was Dan Livingston, the troop's senior patrol leader. He had just finished checking the campsite and was now putting out the campfire. Being the top Scout meant added responsibility, but Dan didn't mind. He was a born leader. It came naturally to him. After he finished, it was time to take a walk to the shower house and prepare for a night's rest. The troop had taken a campsite far back from the others in a primitive area of a state park, so he had to walk a good distance.

The cool, crisp air was filled with the scents and sounds of the night. Dan's thoughts were of the next day's events as he came upon the hard road that ran along a ridge that led to the main area of the campground. It was quite dark. He could just barely make out the outline of the road's edge. Dan had gone about twenty yards or so when it struck him that something had changed. It was much quieter than it had been only a few moments before. Suddenly, without cause or reason, a chill ran up the spine of the senior patrol leader. He was overtaken by a feeling of apprehension, some sense of foreboding that he couldn't justify. Dan knew he was tired, and dismissed the feeling as silliness on his part, then continued on his way.

In the past Dan had stumbled on a lot of critters while roaming about the woods at night, and some had given him quite a startle. The sudden rustling noise on the side of the road gave him no real concern. It could've been most anything—perhaps a raccoon on its way to the main campgrounds for a late-night snack from some camper's ice chest.

The rustling noise continued. It seemed to be parallel to him. It was then that the apprehension Dan had felt

The Companion

earlier came sweeping over him like a wave. Only this time the feeling cut through him like a knife. A shiver started in the small of his back. By the time it climbed the length of his spinal column, his entire body shook. At the same time, the now unwanted companion moved onto the road directly to Dan's right and seemed to measure its stride against Dan's. Without changing his cadence, Dan's head naturally turned in its direction. But darkness prevailed, and he could see nothing of the intruder. Instinctively he reached for the flashlight in the holster that he wore on his hip. But sensing that whatever it was that walked next to him was of good size, he knew that startling it with the light could prove dangerous if it panicked. So the senior patrol leader decided to forego the light in favor of calming himself and regaining control of his fear.

The sound of its footsteps seemed to ring in the young man's ears. Its breathing was heavy and coarse, almost raspy. A bitter, somewhat rancid odor, much like that of a damp, unkempt animal, filled the air. Dan wouldn't even try to tell you that he was without concern, but somehow he did manage to remain somewhat calm. He tried to maintain his pace as best he could, although maybe somewhat quicker. Dan held his head rigidly straight ahead. He could feel that his body was tight with tension. The urge to bolt was almost overwhelming. Somehow he managed to resist this urge and maintain his now quickened pace.

Now I agree that it may sound strange, but Dan found himself curious as to exactly what his new-found companion was—or wasn't! His fear gave way, at least momentarily, to curiosity. He began to try to decipher what the creature was that walked next to him. The possibility that it was human was quickly dismissed. By the smell, it could have been a large fur-bearing animal, possibly damp from crossing a stream. But then it should have hooves, which, on the hard road, would make a clip-clop sound. It was then that Dan listened to its footsteps, and then his apprehension came flying back! There was definitely clipping noises, which would mean hooves—but there were no clops from hind legs! With bated breath, the young man strained his ears, trying to hear more than two legs. Dan's mouth became dry, his breathing short and gasping. He wondered if the thing could sense the terror that now possessed every cell in his body.

The senior Scout wasn't sure how much farther he had to go until he came into the light of the main campground. At this time panic seemed to take over, and Dan quickened his pace dramatically. To his horror, so did his invisible companion. It stayed directly to the right. Dan's heart felt as if it would pound right through his chest. Dan's breathing was very short and gaspy, almost to the point of hyperventilation. Suddenly it occurred to him that its breathing had changed. It was now short and deep, sort of a snorting, as if it had become aggravated.

The young man's terror was now complete. It is uncertain what would have happened if Dan hadn't seen the light of the main camp shining through the woods ahead of him. The light at least gave him some hope, which didn't deter the fear so much as allow Dan to control it somewhat. The Scout concentrated on the light and quickened his pace to a near run. Dan could feel that the enigma had kept pace and remained at his side. Its breathing becoming louder as the pace became faster. Dan could see the light on the road ahead and focused his mind on the fact that he would be safe if he could only make it to the light. With only a few yards to go, his terror-ridden strides were more like leaps. His heart was pounding so hard, Dan was sure it would jump from his chest. His lungs burned with each gasped breath. He found himself urging his body along. Then with only a matter of steps to go . . . all became silent . . . except for his labored breathing and the sound of his footsteps. Dan continued on until he was well into the lighted section of the road. He then stopped and spun around. Dan was sure it was still there in the middle of the road. He was sure that he hadn't heard the creature move off to the side. He stared at the darkness, almost expecting it to suddenly leap out at him, but somehow knowing that it wouldn't. Dan reached for his flashlight and aimed it back down the road. Gritting his teeth to maintain his courage, Dan turned it on!

There was nothing there! The senior Scout swung the light quickly back and forth, but still there was nothing. Dan stood for sometime, breathing heavily and shining the light down the road. Finally he went on to the shower house and tried to soothe his jagged nerves with a very hot, very long shower. As he stood there with the water running over his lowered head, curiosity took over where only moments before there was only fear and terror.

"Why didn't I shine my light on it sooner?" he asked himself. "At least I would have seen it. I would have known what it was!" Dan became angry and chastised himself for being such a coward.

Then it occurred to him that he still had to go back to camp, and that he might encounter it again. All he had to do was walk back in the dark just as he had come. Surely it would still be there. Dan literally jumped from the shower and dressed. With his hair still wet, the troop's senior patrol leader headed back to camp.

But Dan never saw it again. To this day he still has no idea what it was. Every now and then he thinks about it, usually while walking the woods at night. He's still curious as to what it could have been. Dan didn't get to see it on his way back to camp that night. Of course, he knew he wouldn't if he had a light on. He had a very good light; he'd just put new batteries in it that day. Dan figures they burned out . . . sometime before dawn.

Story Outline

I. After the troop settles in for the night, the senior patrol leader, Dan Livingston, leaves for the main campground to take a shower.

II. Walking along the pitch-black road, Dan suddenly notices that the woods have become quieter than before.

III. The feeling of apprehension is intensified when he becomes aware of a sudden rustling noise along the side of the road.

IV. A shiver of fear starts in the small of his back and climbs the length of his spinal column as the unwanted companion moves onto the road directly to his right and seems to take up his stride.

V. He looks in the direction of the noise, but he can see nothing of the intruder in the inky blackness of the night.

VI. He instinctively reaches for his flashlight, but he hesitates using it for fear that he might startle the creature, which could prove dangerous if it panicked.

VII. The creature's breathing is heavy, and the odor of a damp animal fills the air.

VIII. As Dan tensely walks on, he struggles to keep his speed even.

IX. He tries to imagine what sort of creature is walking alongside him in the dark.

X. His ears strain to study the footsteps of the animal—he hears a clipping noise of hooves, but no clops from hind legs.

XI. Terribly frightened, he quickens his pace— and so does his nighttime companion.

XII. The creature starts snorting, as if aggravated by the quickened pace.

XIII. The light of the main camp becomes visible in the distance, providing Dan some hope.

XIV. The Scout concentrates on the light and quickens his pace to a near run.

XV. The creature keeps pace—Dan breathes in gasps and his heart pounds as he runs desperately for the safety of the main camp.

XVI. With only steps to go, Dan suddenly realizes the only sound he hears is his own labored breathing.

XVII. He stops and spins around. Seeing nothing, he aims his flashlight and turns it on . . . There is nothing there!

XVIII. At first relieved, Dan's curiosity increases; he becomes angry with himself because he did not shine his light on the creature to learn its identity.

XIX. He leaves the shower and eagerly looks forward to the adventure of returning to camp.

XX. But he never sees the creature. Of course, he knows he won't see it if he uses his flashlight—and his flashlight probably does not burn itself out until nearly dawn.

15

THE MINNESOTA MAGGOT OF DEATH

as told by Doc Forgey

This old folk tale is simple, yet it readily conjures up thoughts of an evil and hideous ghoulie—one that becomes particularly dreadful around a campfire, deep in the woods on some dark night. Try to personalize the introduction, much as I have.

During a recent visit with my old canoe buddy, Cliff Jacobson, I was shown an overgrown church cemetery near his hometown of Hastings, Minnesota. Perhaps the most loathsome and terrifying apparition ever seen there was a maggoty creature that was said to have haunted this little Minnesota churchyard years ago.

The first man to see it was Mr. Thomas, the baker. He was passing the graveyard on his way home on a bright moonlit night when his attention was caught by a large blob of luminous ooze, issuing from the fresh grave of a recently dead villager names Jenkins. The giant, ugly glowworm wriggled and grew bigger as it slithered from the ground. Repulsed and horrified, Thomas was nevertheless fascinated by the creature. It looked exactly like a giant glowing maggot. He never liked cutting through the cemetery by himself, so it took all of the courage that he could muster to even watch the monster. When he saw its eyes, he was forced to look away from it, for the evil creature stared in a strangely human fashion. Its hideous face seemed to recognize him, yet it was decidedly not human—it was a creature from beyond the grave that exuded pure evil.

Thomas followed the ghastly monster as it slithered along the ground, leaving a gleaming trail of disgusting slime in its wake. The maggot wriggled along the paths between the tombstones and soon reached the edge of the graveyard. Thomas followed the slimy trail until it ended at the door of the village postmaster's house nearby.

The next day Thomas told his wife and his best friend about the incredible experience. That night the three of them went to the cemetery to see if they could discover anything more about the hideous monster. Suddenly the ground above Jenkins's grave quivered and the dreadful creature oozed forth. The three friends followed at a distance until it disappeared once again at the postmaster's house. The next day the Thomases and their friend were

The Minnesota Maggot of Death

shocked to learn that the postmaster and his entire family had taken ill. Worse, by the time the sun set that night, all members of the family were dead. The perplexed doctor taking care of them decided that they had all died of carbon monoxide poisoning.

Resolved now more than ever to learn about the glowing maggot's origin, Thomas, his wife, and their friend returned to the grave that very night. Again the ground above Jenkins's grave trembled and the glowing maggot poked its slimy head above the surface. The creature slithered up from the grave, glanced in their direction, and then crawled between the tombstones. Following the familiar trail of glowing slime, the three friends followed the trail until it vanished at the house of the village school principal. There was no need for the creature to visit the principal a second time, nor did Thomas have a chance to warn him. The principal became ill in the morning and died before sunset, like the postmaster and his family, of carbon monoxide poisoning.

Now completely frightened and more bewildered than ever, Thomas and his companions decided to return to the graveyard that very night. Almost to their astonishment, nothing happened. They were afraid to tell anyone of their sightings for fear they would be made to look hysterical or even implicated in the deaths. They decided to maintain their nightly vigil at the grave for at least two weeks.

On the tenth night of watching, the creature again emerged from Jenkins's grave, this time slithering purposefully straight toward the Thomas home. The Thomases were horror stricken. Rushing into their house, they grabbed their five-year-old son and rushed him outside. That night they all stayed at their friend's house. In the morning they found their pet dog, Jack, dead—the vet said of carbon monoxide poisoning.

That very night, their hearts filled with anger and fear, Thomas and his wife, accompanied by their friend, went back to the grave site. This time they meant to strike back at the monster. Equipped with a kerosene lantern and shovels, they dug up the grave of the late Mr. Jenkins.

When they struck the coffin, Mrs. Thomas held the lantern, while her husband and his friend pried the lid off. Mrs. Thomas shrieked when she saw the corpse, dropping her lantern. Mr. Thomas and his friend sprang back from the coffin, allowing the lid to slam shut. But before it closed, they could both see that a hideous green glow emanated from it.

The two men then placed a rope around the coffin and dragged it from the graveyard to a nearby field. Taking the now-broken lantern, they poured the remaining kerosene over the coffin and lit it on fire, burning it to cinders. After returning to the cemetery, they filled the grave and covered all traces of their having been there.

The monstrous maggot of death was never seen again. Mr. Thomas later learned that the dead man had been on bad terms with both the postmaster and the school principal. He had never had any trouble with Jenkins, but he remembered with a shudder how the evil glowing maggot had stared at him as it crawled away from the cemetery on its way to perform its hideous deeds.

Story Outline

I. Mr. Thomas passes through the cemetery one night when he sees a hideous blob of luminous ooze wriggle up from a fresh grave.

II. A glowing, monstrous maggot slithers out of the graveyard, leaving a trail of gleaming slime until it disappears into the postmaster's house.

III. Thomas, his wife, and best friend return to the cemetery the next night, and again the glowing maggot slithers from the grave to the postmaster's house.

IV. The next day the postmaster and his entire family take ill and are dead by sunset—the doctor believes from carbon monoxide poisoning.

V. The three companions return to the churchyard the following night and again watch as the glowing maggot leaves the grave and makes its way to the school principal's house.

VI. The school principal becomes ill in the morning and dies before the three friends can warn him. Carbon monoxide poisoning is said to be the cause of the principal's death.

VII. Thoroughly alarmed, yet afraid to look foolish to the authorities, Thomas and his companions watch the cemetery nightly, but nothing happened for ten days.

VIII. When it reappears, the glowing maggot heads directly for the Thomas house. Terrified, they take their son and spend the night at their friend's home.

IX. On returning home they find that their pet dog, which had been left behind in their haste, is dead—the vet says from carbon monoxide poisoning.

X. That night the three friends return to the graveyard and dig up the corpse from Jenkin's grave.

XI. They remove the coffin to a nearby field and burn it to cinders.

XII. They learn that the dead man had hated the postmaster and school principal. He had never had any trouble with Jenkins, but Thomas remembers with a shudder how the evil glowing maggot had stared at him as it crawled away from the cemetery on its way to perform its hideous deeds.

RUNNING WOLF

by Algernon Blackwood

Algernon Blackwood has produced many stories of the occult. Because of his interest in the outdoors, and his experiences canoeing and camping in Canada and Europe, many of these stories deal with the mysterious aspects of deep wilderness. Two of his longer stories that are must reads for outdoorsmen are "The Wendigo" and "The Willows." Both of these stories are rather long, however, and are difficult to tell around a campfire in their entirety. "Running Wolf," however, is an ideal campfire story by the master of the wilderness macabre.

The man who enjoys an adventure outside the general experience of the race, and imparts it to others, must not be surprised if he is taken for either a liar or a fool, as Malcolm Hyde, hotel clerk on a holiday, discovered of course. Nor is *enjoy* the right word to use in describing his emotions; the word he chose was probably *survive*.

When he first set eyes on Medicine Lake, he was struck by its still, sparkling beauty, lying there in the vast Canadian backwoods; next, by its extreme loneliness; and, lastly—a good deal later, this—by its combination of beauty, loneliness, and singular atmosphere, due to the fact that it was the scene of his adventure.

"It's fairly stiff with big fish," said Morton of the Montreal Sporting Club. "Spending your holidays there— up Mattawa way, some fifteen miles west of Stony Creek. You'll have it all to yourself except for an old Indian who's got a shack there. Camp on the east side—if you'll take a tip from me." He then talked for half an hour about the wonderful sport; yet he was not otherwise very communicative and did not suffer questions gladly, Hyde noticed. Nor had he stayed there very long himself. If it was such a paradise as Morton, its discoverer and the most experienced rod in the province, claimed, why had he himself spent only three days there?

"Ran short of grub," was the only explanation offered; but to another friend he had mentioned briefly, "flies," and to a third, so Hyde learned later, he gave the excuse that his half-breed "took sick," necessitating a quick return to civilization.

Hyde, however, cared little for the explanations; his interest in these came later. "Stiff with fish" was the phrase he liked. He took the Canadian Pacific train to Mattawa, laid in his outfit at Stony Creek, and set off thence for the fifteen-mile canoe trip without a care in the world.

Traveling light, the portages did not trouble him; the water was swift and east, the rapids negotiable; everything came his way, as the saying is. Occasionally he saw a big fish making for the deeper pools and was sorely tempted to stop; but he resisted. He pushed on between the immense world of forests that stretched for hundreds of miles, known to deer, bear, moose, and wolf, but strange to any echo of human tread, a deserted and primeval wilderness. The autumn day was calm, the water sang and sparkled, the blue sky hung cloudless over all, ablaze with light. Toward evening he passed an old beaver dam, rounded a little point, and had his first sight of Medicine Lake. He lifted his dripping paddle; the canoe shot with silent glide into calm water. He gave an exclamation of delight, for the loveliness took his breath away.

Though primarily a sportsman, he was not insensible to beauty. The lake formed a crescent, perhaps four miles long, its width between a mile and half a mile. The slanting fold of sunset flooded it. No wind stirred its crystal surface. Here it had lain since the redskins' god first made it; here it would lie until he dried it up again. Towering spruce and hemlock trooped to its very edge, majestic cedars leaned down as if to drink, crimson sumacs shone in fiery patches, and maples gleamed orange and red beyond belief. The air was like wine, with the silence of a dream.

It was here the red men formerly "made medicine," with all the wild ritual and tribal ceremony of the ancient day. But it was of Morton, rather than of Indians, that Hyde thought. If this lonely, hidden paradise was really stiff with big fish, he owed a lot to Morton for the information. Peace invaded him, but the excitement of the hunter lay below.

He looked about him with quick, practiced eyes for a camping place before the sun sank below the forests and the half-light came. The Indian's shack, lying in full sunshine on the eastern shore, he found at once; but the trees lay too thick about it for comfort, nor did he wish to be so close to its inhabitant. Upon the opposite side, however, an ideal clearing offered. This lay already in shadow, the huge forest darkening it toward evening; but the open space attracted. He paddled over quickly and examined it. The ground was hard and dry, he found, and a little brook ran tinkling down one side of it onto the lake. This out fall, too, would be a good fishing spot. Also, it was sheltered. A few low willows marked the mouth.

An experienced camper soon makes up his mind. It was a perfect site, and some charred logs, with traces of former fires, proved that he was not the first to think so. Hyde was delighted. Then, suddenly, disappointment came to tinge his pleasure. His kit was landed, and preparations for putting up the tent were begun, when he recalled a detail that excitement had so far kept in the background of his mind—Morton's advice. But not Morton's only, for the storekeeper at Stony Creek had reinforced it. The big fellow with a straggling moustache and stooping shoulders, dressed in shirt and trousers, had handed him out a final sentence with the bacon, flour, condensed milk, and sugar. He had repeated Morton's half-forgotten words:

"Put your tent on the east shore, I should," he had said at parting.

He remembered Morton, too, apparently. "A short-ish fellow, brown as an Indian and fairly smelling of the woods. Traveling with Jake, the half-breed." That assuredly was Morton. "Didn't stay long, now, did he," he added to himself in a reflective tone.

"Going Windy Lake way, are yer? Or Ten Mile Water, maybe?" he had first inquired of Hyde.

"Medicine Lake."

"Is that so?" the man said, as though he doubted it for some obscure reason. He pulled at his ragged moustache a moment. "Is that so, now?" he repeated. And the final words followed him downstream after a considerable pause—the advice about the best shore on which to put his tent.

All this now suddenly flashed back upon Hyde's mind with a tinge of disappointment and annoyance, for when two experienced men agreed, their opinion was not to be lightly disregarded. He wished he had asked the storekeeper for many details. He looked about him, he reflected, he hesitated. His ideal camping ground lay certainly on the forbidden shore. What in the world, he wondered, could be the objection to it?

But light was fading; he must decide quickly one way or the other. After staring at his unpacked dunnage, and the tent, already half erected, he made up his mind with a muttered expression that consigned both Morton and the storekeeper to less pleasant places. "They must have some reason," he growled to himself. "Fellows like that usually know what they're talking about. I guess I'd better shift over to the other side—for tonight, at any rate."

He glanced across the water before actually reloading. No smoke rose from the Indian's shack. He had seen no sign of a canoe. The man, he decided, was away. Reluctantly, then, he left the good camping ground and paddled across the lake, and half an hour later his tent was up, firewood collected, and two small trout were already caught for supper. But the bigger fish, he knew lay waiting for him on the other side by the little out fall, and he fell asleep at length on his bed of balsam boughs, annoyed and disappointed, yet wondering how a mere sentence could have persuaded him so easily against his own better judgment. He slept like the dead; the sun was well up before he stirred.

But his morning mood was a very different one. The brilliant light, the peace, the intoxicating air, all this was too exhilarating for his mind to harbor foolish fancies, and he marveled that he could have been so weak the night before. No hesitation lay in him anywhere. He struck camp immediately after breakfast, paddled back across the strip of shining water, and quickly settled in upon the forbidden shore, as he now called it, with a contemptuous grin. And the more he saw of the spot, the better he liked it. There was plenty of wood, running water to drink, an open space about the tent, and there were no flies. The fishing, moreover, was magnificent. Morton's description was fully justified, and "stiff with big fish" for once was not exaggeration.

The useless hours of the early afternoon he passed dozing in the sun, or wandering through the underbrush beyond the camp. He found no sign of anything unusual. He bathed in a cool, deep pool; he reveled in the lonely little paradise. Lonely it certainly was, but loneliness was part of its charm; the stillness, the peace, the isolation of this beautiful backwoods lake delighted him. The silence was divine. He was entirely satisfied.

After a brew of tea, he strolled toward evening along the shore, looking for the first sign of a rising fish. A faint ripple on the water, with the lengthening shadows, made good conditions. Plop followed plop, as the big fellows rose, snatched at their food, and vanished into the depths. He hurried back. Ten minutes later he had taken his rods and was gliding cautiously in the canoe through the quiet water.

So good was the sport, indeed, and so quickly did the big trout pile up in the bottom of the canoe, that despite the growing lateness, he found it hard to tear himself away. "One more," he said, "and then I really will go." He landed that "one more," and the evening was curiously disturbed. He became abruptly aware that someone watched him. A pair of eyes, it seemed, was fixed upon him from some point in the surrounding shadows.

Thus, at least, he interpreted the odd disturbance in his happy mood; for thus he felt it. The feeling stole over him without the slightest warning. He was not alone. The slippery big trout dropped from his fingers. He sat motionless and stared about him.

Nothing stirred; the ripple on the lake had died away; there was no wind; the forest lay a single purple mass of shadow; the yellow sky, fast fading, threw reflections that troubled the eye and made distances uncertain. But there was no sound, no movement; he saw no figure anywhere. Yet he knew that someone watched him, and a wave of quiet unreasoning terror gripped him. The nose of the canoe was against the bank. In a moment, and instinctively, he shoved it off and paddled into deeper water. The watcher, it came to him also instinctively, was quite close to him on the bank. But where? And who? Was it the Indian?

Here, in deeper water, and some twenty yards from the shore, he paused and strained both sight and hearing to find some possible clue. He felt half ashamed, now that the first strange feeling passed a little. But the certainty remained. Absurd as it was, he felt positive that someone watched him with concentrated and intent regard. Every fiber in his being told him so; and though he could discover no figure, no new outline on the shore, he could even have sworn in which clump of willow bushes the hidden person crouched and stared. His attention seemed drawn to that particular clump.

The water dripped slowly from his paddle, now lying across the thwarts. There was no other sound. The canvas of his tent gleamed dimly. A star or two were out. He waited. Nothing happened.

Then, as suddenly as it had come, the feeling passed, and he knew that the person who had been watching him intently had gone. It was as if a current had been turned off; the normal world flowed back; the landscape emptied as if someone had left a room. The disagreeable feeling left him at the same time, so that he instantly turned the canoe in the shore again, landed, and paddle in hand, went over to examine the clump of willows he had singled out as the place of concealment. There was no one there, of course, nor any trace of recent human occupancy. No leaves, no branches stirred, nor was a single twig displaced; his keen and practiced sight detected no sign of tracks upon the ground. Yet, for all that, he felt positive that a little time ago someone had crouched among these very leaves and watched him. He remained absolutely convinced of it. The watcher, whether Indian hunter, stray lumberman, or wandering half-breed, had now withdrawn, a search was useless, and dusk was falling. He returned to his little camp, more disturbed perhaps than he cared to acknowledge. He cooked his supper, hung up his catch on a string, so that no prowling animal could get at it during the night, and prepared to make himself comfortable until bedtime. Unconsciously, he built a bigger fire than usual, and found himself peering over his pipe into the deep shadows beyond the firelight, straining his ears to catch the slightest sound. He remained generally on the alert in a way that was new to him.

A man under such conditions and in such a place need not know discomfort until the sense of loneliness strikes him as too vivid a reality. Loneliness in a backwoods camp brings charm, pleasure, and a happy sense of calm until, and unless, it comes too near. It should remain an ingredient only among other conditions; it should not be directly, vividly noticed. Once it has crept within short range, however, it may easily cross the narrow line between comfort and discomfort, and darkness is an undesirable time for the transition. A curious dread may easily follow—the dread lest the loneliness suddenly be disturbed, and the solitary human feel himself open to attack.

For Hyde, now, this transition had been already accomplished; the too intimate sense of his loneliness had shifted abruptly into the worst condition of no longer being quite alone. It was an awkward moment, and the hotel clerk realized his position exactly. He did not quite like it. He sat there, with his back to the blazing logs, a very visible object in the light, while all about him the darkness of the forest lay like an impenetrable wall. He could not see a yard beyond the small circle of his campfire; the silence about him was like the silence of the dead. No leaf rustled, no wave lapped; he himself sat motionless as a log.

Then again he became suddenly aware that the person who watched him had returned, and the same intent and concentrated gaze as before was fixed upon him where he lay. There was no warning; he heard no stealthy tread or snapping of dry twigs, yet the owner of those steady eyes was very close to him, probably not a dozen feet away. This sense of proximity was overwhelming.

It was unquestionable that a shiver ran down his spine. This time, moreover, he felt positive that the man crouched just beyond the firelight, the distance he himself could see being nicely calculated, was straight in front of him. For some minutes he sat without stirring a single muscle, yet with each muscle ready and alert, straining his eyes in vain to pierce the darkness, he only succeeded in dazzling his sight with the reflected light. Then, as he shifted his position slowly, his heart gave two big thumps against his ribs and the hair seemed to rise on his scalp with the sense of cold that gave him goose flesh. In the darkness facing him he saw two small and greenish circles that were certainly a pair of eyes, yet not the eyes of an Indian hunter, or of any human being. It was a pair of animal eyes that stared so fixedly at him out of the night. And his certainty had an immediate and natural effect upon him.

For, at the menace of those eyes, the fears of millions of lone hunters since the dawn of time woke in him. Hotel clerk though he was, heredity surged through him in an automatic wave of instinct. His hand groped for a weapon. His fingers fell on the iron head of his small camp ax, and at once he was himself again. Confidence returned; the vague, superstitious dread was gone. This was a bear or wolf that smelled his catch and had come to steal it. With beings of this sort he knew instinctively how to deal, yet admitting, by this very instinct, that his original dread had been of quite another kind.

"I'll damned quick find out what it is," he exclaimed aloud, and snatching a burning brand from the fire, he hurled it with good aim straight at the eyes of the beast before him.

The bit of pitch-pine fell in a shower of sparks that lit the dry grass this side of the animal, flared up in a moment, then died quickly down again. But in the instant of bright illumination he saw clearly what his unwelcome visitor was. A big timber wolf sat on its hindquarters, staring steadily at him through the firelight. He saw its legs and shoulders, he saw also the big hemlock trunks lit up behind it and the willow scrub on each side. It formed a vivid, clear-cut picture shown in clear detail by the momentary blaze. To his amazement, however, the wolf did not turn and bolt away from the burning log, but withdrew a few yards only, and sat there again on its haunches, staring, staring as before. Heavens, how it stared! He "shooed" it, but without effect; it did not budge. He did not waste another good log on it, for his fear was dissipated now; a timber wolf was a timber wolf, and it might sit there as long as it pleased, provided it did not try to steal his catch. No alarm was in him anymore. He knew that wolves were harmless in the summer and autumn and even when "packed" in the winter, they would attack a man only when suffering desperate hunger. So he lay and watched the beast, threw bits of stick in its direction, even talked to it, wondering only why it never moved. "You can stay there forever, if you like," he remarked to it aloud, "for you cannot get at my fish, and the rest of the grub I shall take in my tent with me!"

The creature blinked its bright green eyes, but made no move.

Why, then, if his fear was gone, did he think of certain things as he rolled himself in the Hudson Bay blankets before going to sleep? The immobility of the animal was strange, its refusal to turn and bolt was still stranger. Never before had he known a wild creature that was not afraid of fire. Why did it sit and watch him, as with purpose in its gleaming eyes? How had he felt its presence earlier and instantly? A timber wolf, especially a solitary wolf, was a timid thing, yet this one feared neither man nor fire. Now, as he lay there wrapped in his blankets inside the cozy tent, it sat outside beneath the stars, beside the fading embers, the wind chilly in its fur, the ground cooling beneath its planted paws, watching him, steadily watching him, perhaps until the dawn.

It was unusual, it was strange. Having neither imagination nor tradition, he called upon no store of racial visions. Matter of fact, a hotel clerk on a fishing holiday, he lay there in his blankets, merely wondering and puzzled. A timber wolf was a timber wolf and nothing more. Yet this timber wolf—the idea haunted him—was different. In a word, the deeper part of his original uneasiness remained. He tossed about, he shivered sometimes in his broken sleep; he did not go out to see, but he woke early and unrefreshed.

Again with the sunshine and the morning wind, however, the incident of the night before was forgotten, almost unreal. His hunting zeal was uppermost. The tea and fish were delicious, his pipe had never tasted so good, the glory of this lonely lake amid primeval forests went to his head a little; he was a hunter before the Lord, and nothing else. He tried the edge of the lake, and in the excitement of playing a big fish, knew suddenly that it, the wolf, was there. He paused with the rod, exactly as if struck. He looked about him, he looked in a definite direction. The brilliant sunshine made every smallest detail clear and sharp—boulders of granite, burned stems, crimson sumac, pebbles along the shore in neat, separate detail—without revealing where the watcher hid. Then, his sight wandering farther inshore among the tangled undergrowth, he suddenly picked up the familiar, half-expected outline. The wolf was lying behind a granite boulder, so that only the head, the muzzle, and the eyes were visible. It merged in its background. Had he not known it was a wolf, he could never separate it from the landscape. The eyes shone in the sunlight.

There it lay. He looked straight at it. Their eyes, in fact, actually met full and square. "Great Scott!" he exclaimed aloud. "Why, it's like looking at a human being!"

From that moment, unwittingly, he established a singular personal relation with the beast. And what followed confirmed this undesirable impression, for the animal rose instantly and came down in leisurely fashion to the shore, where it stood looking back at him. It stood and stared into his eyes like some great wild dog so that he was aware of a new and almost incredible sensation—that it courted recognition.

"Well! Well!" he exclaimed again, relieving his feelings by addressing it aloud. "If this doesn't beat everything I ever saw! What d'you want anyway?"

He examined it now more carefully. He had never seen a wolf so big before; it was a tremendous beast, a nasty customer to tackle, he reflected, if it ever came to that. It stood there absolutely fearless and full of confidence. In the clear sunlight he took in every detail of it—a huge, shaggy, lean-flanked timber wolf, its wicked eyes staring straight into his own, almost with a kind of purpose in them. He saw its great jaws, its teeth, and its tongue hung out, dropping saliva a little. And yet the idea of its savagery, its fierceness, was very little in him.

He was amazed and puzzled beyond belief. He wished the Indian would come back. He did not understand this strange behavior in an animal. Its eyes, the odd expression in them, gave him a queer, unusual, difficult feeling. *Had his nerves gone wrong?* he almost wondered.

The beast stood on the shore and looked at him. He wished for the first time that he had brought a rifle. With a resounding smack he brought his paddle down flat upon the water, using all his strength, till the echoes rang as from a pistol shot that was audible from one end of the lake to the other. The wolf never stirred. He shouted, but the beast remained unmoved. He blinked his eyes, speaking as to a dog, a domestic animal, a creature accustomed to human ways. It blinked its eyes in return.

At length, increasing his distance from the shore, he continued fishing, and the excitement of the marvelous sport held his attention—his surface attention, at any rate. At times he almost forgot the attendant beast; yet whenever he looked up, he saw it there. And worse: When he slowly paddled home again, he observed it trotting along the shore as though to keep him company. Crossing a little bay, he spurted, hoping to reach the other point before his undesired and undesirable attendant. Instantly the brute broke into that rapid, tireless lope that, except on ice, can run down anything on four legs in the woods. When he reached the distant point, the wolf was waiting for him. He raised his paddle from the water, pausing a moment for reflection; for his very close attention—there were dusk and night yet to come—he certainly did not relish. His camp was near; he had to land; he felt uncomfortable even in the sunshine of broad day, when, to his keen relief, about a half mile from the tent, he saw the creature suddenly stop and sit down in the open. He waited a moment, then paddled on. It did not follow. There was no attempt to move; it merely sat and watched him. After a few hundred yards, he looked back. It was still sitting where he left it. And the absurd, yet significant, feeling came to him that the beast divined his thought, his

Running Wolf

anxiety, his dread, and was now showing him, as well as it could, that it entertained no hostile feeling and did not meditate attack.

He turned the canoe toward the shore; he landed; he cooked his supper in the dusk; the animal made no sign. Not far away it certainly lay watching, but did not advance, and to Hyde, observant now in a new way, came one sharp, vivid reminder of the strange atmosphere into which his commonplace personality had strayed: He suddenly recalled that his relations with the beast, already established, had progressed distinctly a stage further. This startled him, yet without the accompanying alarm he must certainly have felt twenty-four hours before. He had an understanding with the wolf. He was aware of friendly thoughts toward it. He even went so far as to set out a few big fish on the spot where he had first seen it sitting the previous night. "If he comes," he thought, "he is welcome to them. I've got plenty, anyway." He thought of it now as "he."

Yet the wolf made no appearance until he was in the act of entering his tent a good deal later. It was close to ten o'clock, whereas nine was his hour, and late at that, for turning in. He had, therefore, unconsciously been waiting for him. Then, as he was closing the flap, he saw the eyes close to where he had placed the fish. He waited, hiding himself, and expected to hear sounds of munching jaws; but all was silent. Only the eyes glowed steadily out of the background of pitch darkness. He closed the flap. He had no slightest fear. In ten minutes he was sound asleep.

He could not have slept very long, for when he woke up he could see the shine of a faint red light through the canvas, and the fire had not died down completely. He rose and cautiously peeped out. The air was very cold, he saw his breath. But he also saw the wolf, for it had come in, and was sitting by the dying embers, not two yards away from where he crouched behind the flap. And this time, at these very close quarters, there was something in the attitude of the big wild thing that caught his attention with a vivid thrill of startled surprise and a sudden shock of cold that held him spellbound. He stared, unable to believe his eyes, for the wolf's attitude conveyed to him something familiar that at first he was unable to explain. Its pose reached him in the terms of another thing with which he was entirely at home. What was it? Did his senses betray him? Was he still asleep and dreaming?

Then, suddenly, with a start of uncanny recognition, he knew. Its attitude was that of a dog. Having found the clue, his mind then made an awful leap. For it was, after all, no dog its appearance aped, but something nearer to himself, and more familiar still. Good heavens! It sat there with a pose, the attitude, the gesture in repose of something almost human. And then, with a second shock of biting wonder, it came to him like a revelation. The wolf sat beside that campfire as a man might sit.

Before he could weigh his extraordinary discovery, before he could examine it in detail or with care, the animal, sitting in this ghastly fashion, seemed to feel his eyes fixed on it. It slowly turned and looked him in the face, and for the first time Hyde felt full-blooded superstitious fear flood through his entire being. He seemed transfixed with that nameless terror that is said to attack human beings who suddenly face the dead, finding themselves bereft of speech and movement. This movement of paralysis certainly occurred. Its passing, however, was singular as its advent. For almost at once he was aware of something beyond and above this mockery of human attitude and pose, something that ran along unaccustomed nerves and reached his feeling, even perhaps his heart. The revulsion was extraordinary, its result still more extraordinary and unexpected. Yet the fact remains. He was aware of another thing that had the effect of stilling his terror as soon as it was born. He was aware of appeal, silent, half expressed, yet vastly pathetic. He saw in the savage eyes a beseeching, even a yearning, expression that changed his mood as by magic from dread to natural sympathy. The great gray brute, symbol of cruel ferocity, sat there beside his dying fire and appealed for help.

The gulf betwixt animal and human seemed in that instant bridged. It was, of course, incredible. Hyde, sleep still possibly clinging to his inner being with the shades and half shapes of dreams yet about his soul, acknowledged, how he knew not, the amazing fact. He found himself nodding to the brute in half consent, and instantly, without more ado, the lean gray shape rose like a wraith and trotted off swiftly, but with stealthy tread, into the background of the night.

When Hyde woke in the morning, his first impression was that he must have dreamed the entire incident. His practical nature asserted itself. There was a bite in the fresh autumn air; the bright sun allowed no half lights anywhere; he felt brisk in mind and body. Reviewing what had happened, he came to the conclusion that it was utterly vain to speculate; no possible explanation of the animal's behavior occurred to him. He was dealing with something entirely outside his experience. His fear, however, had completely left him. The odd sense of friendliness remained. The beast had a definite purpose, and he himself was included in that purpose. His sympathy held good.

But with the sympathy there was also an intense curiosity. "If it shows itself again," he told himself, "I'll go up close and find out what it wants." The fish laid out the night before had not been touched.

It must have been a full hour after breakfast when he next saw the brute; it was standing on the edge of the clearing, looking at him in the way that had now become familiar. Hyde immediately picked up his ax and advanced toward it boldly, keeping his eyes fixed straight upon its own. There was a nervousness in him, but kept well under, nothing betrayed it; step by step he drew nearer until some ten yards separated them. The wolf had not stirred a single muscle as yet. Its jaw hung open, its eyes observed him intently; it allowed him to approach without a sign of what its mood might be. Then, with these ten yards between them, it turned abruptly and moved slowly off, looking back first over one shoulder and then over the other, exactly as a dog might do, to see if he was following.

A singular journey it was they made together, animal and man. The trees surrounded them at once, for they left the lake behind them, entering the tangled bush beyond. The beast, Hyde noticed, obviously picked the easiest track for him to follow; for obstacles that meant nothing to the four-legged expert, yet were difficult for a man, were carefully avoided with an almost uncanny skill, while yet the general direction was accurately kept. Occasionally there were windfalls to be surmounted; but though the wolf bounded over these with ease, it was always waiting for the man on the other side after he had laboriously climbed over. Deeper and deeper into the heart of the lonely forest they penetrated in this singular fashion, cutting across the arc of the lake's crescent, it seemed to Hyde; for after two miles or so, he recognized the big rocky bluff he had seen from his camp, one side of it falling sheer into the water; it was probably the spot, he imagined, where the Indians held their medicine-making ceremonies, for it stood out in isolated fashion, and its top formed a private plateau not easy of access. And it was here, close to a big spruce at the foot of the bluff upon the forest side, that the wolf stopped suddenly and for the first time since its appearance gave audible expression to its feelings. It sat down on its haunches, lifted its muzzle with open jaws, and gave vent to a subdued and long-drawn howl that was more like the wail of a dog than the fierce barking cry associated with a wolf.

By this time Hyde had lost not only fear, but caution too; nor, oddly enough, did this warning howl revive a sign of unwelcome emotion in him. In that curious sound he detected the same message that the eyes conveyed—an appeal for help. He paused, nevertheless, a little startled, and while the wolf sat waiting for him, he looked about him quickly. There was young timber here; it had once been a small clearing, evidently. Ax and fire had done their work, but there was evidence to an experienced eye that it was Indians and not white men who had once been busy here. Some part of the medicine ritual, doubtless, took place in the little clearing, thought the man, as he advanced again toward his patient leader. The end of their queer journey, he felt, was close at hand.

He had not taken two steps before the animal got up and moved very slowly in the direction of some low bushes that formed a clump just beyond. It entered these, first looking back to make sure that its companion watched. The bushes hid it; a moment later it emerged again. Twice it performed this pantomime, each time, as it reappeared, standing still and staring at the man with as distinct an expression of appeal in the eyes as an animal may compass, probably. Its excitement, meanwhile, certainly increased, and this excitement was, with equal certainty, communicated to the man. Hyde made up his mind quickly. Gripping his ax tightly, and ready to use it at the first hint of malice, he moved slowly nearer to the bushes, wondering with something of a tremor what would happen.

If he expected to be startled, his expectation was at once fulfilled; but it was the behavior of the beast that made him jump. It positively frisked about him like a happy puppy dog. It frisked for joy. Its excitement was intense, yet from its open mouth no sound was audible. With a sudden leap, then, it bounded past him into the clump of bushes, against whose very edge he stood, and began scraping vigorously at the ground. Hyde stood and stared, amazement and interest now banishing all his nervousness, even when the beast, in its violent scraping, actually touched his body with its own. He had, perhaps, the feeling that he was in a dream, one of those fantastic dreams in which things may happen without involving an adequate surprise; for otherwise the manner of scraping and scratching at the ground must have seemed an impossible phenomenon. No wolf, no dog certainly, used its paws in the way those paws were working. Hyde had the odd, distressing sensation that it was hands, not paws, he watched. And yet, somehow, the natural, adequate surprise he should have felt was absent. The strange action seemed not entirely unnatural. In his heart some deep hidden spring of sympathy and pity stirred instead. He was aware of pathos.

The wolf stopped in its task and looked up into his face. Hyde acted without hesitation then. Afterward he was wholly at a loss to explain his conduct. It seemed he knew what to do, divined what was asked, expected of him. Between his mind and the dumb desire yearning through the savage animal, there was intelligent and intelligible communication. He cut a stake and sharpened it, for the stones would blunt his ax edge. He entered the clump of bushes to complete the digging his four-legged companion had begun. And while he worked, though he did not forget the close proximity of the wolf, he paid no attention to it; often his back was turned as he stooped over the laborious clearing away of the hard earth; no uneasiness or sense of danger was in him anymore. The wolf sat outside the clump and watched the operations. Its concentrated attention, its patience, its intense eagerness, the gentleness and docility of the gray, fierce, and probably hungry brute, its obvious pleasure and satisfaction, too, at having won the human to its mysterious purpose—these were colors in the strange picture that Hyde thought of later when dealing with the human herd in his hotel again. At that moment he was chiefly aware of pathos and affection. The whole business was, of course, not to be believed, but that discovery came later, too, when telling it to others.

The digging continued for fully half an hour before his labor was rewarded by the discovery of a small whitish object. He picked it up and examined it—the finger bone of a man. Other discoveries then followed quickly and in quantity. The cache was laid bare. He collected nearly the complete skeleton. The skull, however, he found last, and might not have found at all but for the guidance of this strangely alert companion. It lay some few yards away from the central hole now dug, and the wolf stood nuzzling the ground with his nose before Hyde understood that he was meant to dig exactly in that spot for it. Between the beast's very paws his stake struck hard upon it. He scraped the earth from the bone and examined it carefully. It was perfect, save for the fact that some wild animal had gnawed it, the teeth marks being still plainly visible. Close beside it lay the rusty iron head of a tomahawk. This and the smallness of the bones confirmed him in his judgment that it was the skeleton not of a white man, but of an Indian.

During the excitement of the discovery of the bones one by one, and finally the skull, but more especially, during the period of intense interest while Hyde was examining them, he had paid little if any attention to the wolf. He was aware that it sat and watched him, never moving its keen eyes for a single moment from the actual operations, but sign or movement it made none at all. He knew that it was pleased and satisfied, he knew also that he had now fulfilled its purpose in a great measure. The further intuition that now came to him, derived, he felt positive, from his companion's dumb desire, was perhaps the cream of the entire experience to him. Gathering the bones together in his coat, he carried them, together with the tomahawk, to the foot of the big spruce where the animal had first stopped. His leg actually touched the creature's muzzle as he passed. It turned its head to watch, but did not follow, nor did it move a muscle while he prepared the platform of boughs upon which he then laid the poor worn bones of the Indian who had been killed, doubt-less, in sudden attack or ambush, and to whose remains had been denied the last grace of proper tribal burial. He wrapped the bones in the bark; he laid the tomahawk beside the skull; he lit the circular fire round the pyre; and the smoke rose upward into the clear bright sunshine or the Canadian autumn morning till it was lost among the mighty trees overhead.

In the moment before actually lighting the little fire he had turned to note what his companion did. It sat five yards away, he saw, gazing intently, and one of its front paws was raised a little from the ground. It made no sign of any kind. He finished the work, becoming so absorbed in it that he had eyes for nothing but the tending and guarding of his careful ceremonial fire. It was only when the platform of boughs collapsed, laying their charred burden gently on the fragrant earth among the soft wood ashes, that he turned again, as though to show the wolf what he had done, and seek, perhaps, some look of sat-isfaction in its curiously expressive eyes. But the place he searched was empty. The wolf had gone.

He did not see it again; it gave no sign of its presence anywhere, he was not watched. He fished as before, wandered through bush about his camp, sat smoking round his fire after dark, and slept peacefully in his cozy little tent. He was not disturbed. No howl was ever audible in the distant forest, no twig snapped beneath a stealthy tread, he saw no eyes. The wolf that behaved like a man had gone forever.

It was the day before he left that Hyde, noticing smoke rising from the shack across the lake, paddled over to exchange a word or two with the Indian, who evidently now returned. The Indian came down to meet him as he landed, but it was soon plain that he spoke very little English. He emitted the familiar grunts at first; then bit by bit Hyde stirred his limited vocabulary into action. The net result, however, was slight enough, though it was certainly direct:

"You camp there?" the man asked, pointing to the other side.

"Yes."

"Wolf come?"

"Yes."

"You see wolf?"

"Yes."

The Indian stared at him fixedly a moment, a keen, wondering look upon his coppery, creased face.

"You 'fraid wolf?" he asked after a moment's pause.

"No," replied Hyde, truthfully. He knew it was useless to ask questions of his own; though he was eager for information, the other would have told him nothing. It was sheer luck that the man had touched on the subject at all, and Hyde realized that his own best role was merely to answer, but to ask no questions. Then, suddenly, the Indian became voluble. There was awe in his voice and manner.

"Him no wolf. Him big medicine wolf. Him spirit wolf."

Whereupon he drank the tea the other had brewed for him, closed his lips tightly, and said no more. His outline was discernible on the shore, rigid and motionless, an hour later, when Hyde's canoe turned the corner of the lake three miles away and landed to make the portages up the first rapid of his homeward stream.

It was Morton who, after persuasion, supplied further details of what he called the legend. Some hundred years before, the tribe that lived in the territory beyond the lake began their annual medicine-making ceremonies on the big rocky bluff at the northern end; but no medicine could be made. The spirits, declared the chief medicine man, would not answer. They were offended. An investigation followed. It was discovered that a young brave had recently killed a wolf, a thing strictly forbidden, since the wolf was the totem animal of the tribe. "To make matters worse, the name of the guilty man was Running Wolf. The offense was unpardonable; the man was cursed and driven from the tribe:

"Go out. Wander alone among the woods, and if we see you we slay you. Your bones shall be scattered in the forest, and your spirit shall not enter the Happy Hunting Grounds till one of another race shall find and bury them."

"Which meant," explained Morton laconically, his only comment on the story, "probably forever."

Story Outline

I. Morton of the Montreal Sporting Club tells Malcom Hyde of a great fishing place—Medicine Lake—a place that he has never returned to even though he spoke of the fishing enthusiastically. Hyde is told in passing to camp near an Indian's cabin on the east side of the lake.

II. On the way to the lake, Hyde stops by a general store and is again told to put his tent on the east shore. The store owner acts surprised that he would even be going to Medicine Lake.

III. After canoeing to the lake, he is delighted with its beauty. He sees a perfect place to camp on the west shore, but because of what everyone else has said, he camps on the east side near the Indian's cabin.

IV. Early the next morning, he canoes over to the perfect camping place on the west shore, sets up camp, and starts serious fishing.

V. He fishes until dusk, when suddenly his happiness is disrupted by the feeling that someone is watching him. Fear suddenly comes over him without warning. He canoes quickly away from the clump of bushes he is close to against the shore, but sees nothing. The feeling leaves.

VI. He returns to the shore and checks the clump of bushes, but sees no evidence of any animal or human.

VII. If possible, remember author Algernon Blackwood's comments on loneliness in a backwoods camp, page 187.

VIII. He feels the presence again of something watching him in the dark. Throwing a burning log into the woods, he sees a large timber wolf staring at him. The wolf stays, but he is not afraid of a timber wolf.

IX. The next day while fishing, he senses the strange wolf on the shore. Their eyes meet, and the wolf comes down to the bank. The wolf follows him toward his camp that night, trotting along the lake's edge as he paddles back.

X. That night the wolf again comes to his camp, but this time sits next to the fire—just as a human being would sit.

XI. Hyde decides to find out what the wolf wants. The next day he approaches the wolf, then follows it on a journey through the woods.

XII. At the foot of the large bluff, an area sacred to the ancient Indians, the wolf indicates to him to dig in a certain spot.

XIII. He uncovers a human skeleton, probably the skeleton of an Indian. The wolf also shows him where to find the skull a few yards away.

XIV. He feels compelled to build a funeral pyre. After burning the remains of the skeleton, he turns and finds that the wolf has gone.

XV. He does not see the wolf during the rest of his trip at the lake. The Indian on the other side of the lake sees him during his last day there and tells him that it was no wolf, but a spirit wolf.

XVI. Morton later tells him the legend of the brave called Running Wolf, who had killed a wolf, the totem animal of his tribe. He was condemned to death and to have his spirit wander until one of another race would find his bones and properly bury them.

TATANKA SAPA AND HIS MEDICINE BOW

by David R. Scott

Daniel Hawthorne lived with his father, Joseph, and his mother, Annette, in a tiny one-room log cabin. It was a time when the West was still "wild" and when each step had to be taken with caution. Rumors of "savage" Indian tribes were known by all the squatters in the area, and the people said that if the Indians didn't get you, then the land certainly would. Because of high upbringing, Daniel believed those rumors thoroughly, even though his folks were generally good people who didn't spread falsehoods.

One day while hunting, Daniel came upon an old Indian man lying helplessly in the forest. His first thought was to flee, until he saw how sick the old man really was. His fear quickly passed, and he felt he had no choice other than to help him.

Daniel helped the old man to his feet, and although no words were spoken—at least none that were comprehended by either of the two—a great bonding had taken place. Slowly the Indian, with the help of his new friend, made his way through the forest carrying with him the last of all he possessed. The Indian kept on speaking in a language foreign to Daniel, and Daniel kept telling the old man how much trouble he was going to get into when he got home. On and on the two walked until they could both see the tiny log home. Upon seeing the cabin, the Indian seemed hesitant—almost afraid. Perhaps he had heard equally frightening stories of the "savage" settlers.

Daniel's parents were furious with him for bringing home an Indian. In fact his father wanted to shoot the old man. Daniel ended the dispute by stepping between the two and reminding his father of the lessons that he'd learned.

"If someone is in trouble, no matter who they may be, you help them. Remember what you told me?" Daniel told his father. At that point, the reluctant parents had no choice other than to help the old Indian.

Over the course of the next four weeks, Daniel and the Indian become very close friends. He discovered that the old man's name was Tatanka Sapa, Black Bull. From his bed, Black Bull showed Daniel how to knap arrowheads, set traps, and play traditional Native American games. The two even learned words and sign language from each other's language, but words did not need to be spoken, for theirs was a friendship of the heart. As their friendship grew, however, the Indian continued to sicken.

Before the night of his death, Black Bull signaled for Daniel to come to his side. He reached beneath the bunk and pulled out a large bag made of animal skins and motioned for Daniel to open it. Inside was the most beautiful bow, accompanied by ten meticulously made arrows. He gave the bow and arrows to Daniel and made the sign for *brother,* after which he passed away.

Several weeks went by, and one day Daniel fell asleep after finishing his chores. His mother and father were half a mile away gathering berries in the meadow. What they didn't know was that a grizzly bear was doing the same, keeping a careful eye on the couple at all times. The gnarled old bruin eventually became bored with the two and headed toward the cabin. Annette sensed that something was wrong. No birds were singing, no animals were chatting, even the wind was still. At that moment she saw the large bear enter the partially open door of the cabin.

She and her husband rushed with great speed to save their son, yet they knew they were too far away to get there in time. When they finally reached the front door, they were astounded. There, sprawled out dead on the floor before them, was the great grizzly bear. On the bunk beside the bear lay their son fast asleep.

No one could figure out how the bear had died, for there was no obvious wound. But when Daniel's father was butchering the great beast, he found a beautiful hand-crafted arrowhead embedded deep in its heart.

Quickly he dashed into the cabin where Daniel kept the bow and arrows given to him by the old Indian. The arrowhead retrieved from the bear's heart was a perfect match with the arrows given to Daniel. And when he counted the arrows in the quiver, there were only nine. As for the tenth, it was gone.

Tatanka Sapa and His Medicine Bow

Story Outline

I. Daniel Hawthorne lived on the frontier at a time when Indians were considered dangerous enemies.

II. He finds an ill elderly Indian and brings him home to nurse him back to health, much to Daniel's parents' objections.

III. The Indian returns Daniel's kindness with his friendship and a gift of a medicine bow and ten arrows. Then he dies.

IV. Daniel is asleep in the cabin one day when his parents see a grizzly bear enter the cabin.

V. The frantic parents reach the cabin from their field, only to find the bear dead and Daniel fast asleep.

VI. Upon butchering the bear, Daniel's father finds an arrow has killed the bear and one of the arrows has mysteriously disappeared from the old Indian's quiver while Daniel slept.

SOURCES

Chapter 1, pages 7–19, *The Graveyard Rats,* by Henry Kuttner: Reprinted by permission of Don Congdon Associates, copyright 1939 by Henry Kuttner, renewed 1964.

Chapter 3, pages 28–37, *Gold Tooth,* by Scott E. Power, copyright 1989.

Chapter 4, pages 38–42, *Beneath the Lone Post,* by David R. Scott, copyright 1989.

Chapter 5, pages 43–64, *Lost Face,* by Jack London.

Chapter 8, pages 94–111, *The Indian Head,* by Pat Sherwood, as told by William Forgey.

Chapter 9, pages 112–122, *The Nightmare Trail,* by Scott E Power, copyright 1989.

Chapter 10, pages 123–129, *The Bloody Hand,* Anonymous, as told by William Forgey, public domain.

Chapter 11, pages 130–135, *One Summer Night,* by Ambrose Bierce.

Chapter 12, pages 136–146, *The Stranger,* by Ambrose Bierce.

Chapter 13, pages 147–162, *The Manor,* Sir Walter Scott, as told by Pat Sherwood and William Forgey.

Chapter 14, pages 163–171, *The Companion,* by Pat Sherwood, copyright 1989.

Chapter 16, pages 179–208, *Running Wolf,* by Algernon Blackwood.

Chapter 17, pages 209–213, *Tatanka Sapa and His Medicine Bow,* by David R. Scott, copyright 1989.

ABOUT THE AUTHOR

William W. "Doc" Forgey, M.D., is an outdoorsman and physician from Gary, Indiana. He has been telling ghost stories to children and adults for years. He honed his storytelling skills during his ten years as a Scout leader and on canoeing and camping trips with friends.

In addition to telling tales, Forgey is the editor of *Campfire Stories, Volume 1* and *Campfire Stories, Volume 3,* and is the author of *Wilderness Medicine, Basic Essentials: First Aid,* and *Basic Essentials: Hypothermia,* all published by Globe Pequot Press. He is also a member of the Northern Tier High Adventure Base Advisory Committee for the Boy Scouts of America, a member of the Scouts' National Health and Safety Committee, and is past president of the Wilderness Medical Society.

Finally, he wants to reassure parents that scary stories are fun and not detrimental to children's health!

ABOUT THE ILLUSTRATOR

Paul Hoffman's work graces books of many genres—children's titles, textbooks, short story collections, natural history volumes, and numerous cookbooks. His illustrations can also be found in Globe Pequot Press's *Spooky* series. He lives in Massachusetts.